"Ivy, you ha to die."

Let him go? Had he lost his mind? No. She wasn't letting him go. She needed him alive.

The shooter slammed a new magazine into place and lowered the barrel of his assault rifle. At her. And yet Ivy couldn't seem to let her hand relax. Carson's weight was tearing her apart from the inside. She couldn't let him go. Not again. Not after everything they'd already survived together.

"You can do this. You have to do this, Ivy." Carson stared up at her, those dark eyes as familiar and foreign as she remembered. "I'll be fine."

She released his hand.

K-9 JUSTICE

NICHOLE SEVERN

Harlequin
INTRIGUE

To all the readers who believe love can't conquer injuries.

You're going to hate this book.

Harlequin®
INTRIGUE™

Recycling programs
for this product may
not exist in your area.

ISBN-13: 978-1-335-45740-0

K-9 Justice

Copyright © 2025 by Natascha Jaffa

Harlequin Enterprises ULC
22 Adelaide St. West, 41st Floor
Toronto, Ontario M5H 4E3, Canada
www.Harlequin.com

Printed in Lithuania

MIX
Paper | Supporting
responsible forestry
FSC® C021394

Nichole Severn writes explosive romantic suspense with strong heroines, heroes who dare challenge them and a hell of a lot of guns. She resides with her very supportive and patient husband, as well as her demon spawn, in Utah. When she's not writing, she's constantly injuring herself running, rock climbing, practicing yoga and snowboarding. She loves hearing from readers through her website, www.nicholesevern.com, and on Facebook at nicholesevern.

Books by Nichole Severn

Harlequin Intrigue

New Mexico Guard Dogs

Defenders of Battle Mountain

Visit the Author Profile page at Harlequin.com.

CAST OF CHARACTERS

Ivy Bardot—She founded Socorro Security to battle the cartels the government can't touch, but she never imagined losing a member of her team in the process. With the last operatives of the *Sangre por Sangre* cartel on the run, she's on a mission to find the killer. And the only person she trusts to help is a man on the inside.

Carson Lang—He's been embedded in the cartel for two years since leaving the FBI to find a killer, and now his cover is blown. He has no choice but to partner with Ivy like old times to finish what he started. As the danger draws closer, Carson must make a choice: his cartel family or the partner he's always loved.

Socorro Security—A private military contractor funded by the Pentagon and founded by Ivy Bardot. The country's best defense against New Mexico's most brutal cartel.

Sangre por Sangre—Public enemy number one. This drug cartel has burned entire towns to the ground to get what it wants, and now its members are on the run.

Chapter One

The cartel had come for one of their own.

Ivy Bardot tried not to let the heat get to her, but there was no fighting it. The body had been left in the middle of the desert. Just like the others. A message. For her.

Dark hair splayed out from around a thin face. Wide eyes that had seen so much within the walls of Socorro Security stared into the sky without any life behind them.

The elements had done their job, stripping moisture from the victim's ocher skin and leaving nothing but a thick rawhide behind. *Victim.* That word wasn't supposed to fit. It wasn't supposed to touch anyone on her team. She'd tried to make sure of that since founding Socorro. Every operative was trained to take care of themselves. No matter the circumstance. Search and rescue, emergency protocols, food and supplies in every vehicle, combat training. It didn't matter the face staring back at her had seen more violence and blood out of the field rather than in. Ivy was responsible for all of them.

What had Dr. Piel done wrong?

"That her?" Chief of police Baker Halsey let his shadow cast across the cracked desert floor. Alpine Valley's protector had done his job. He'd taken Ivy's suspicion and run with it. Right out here into the middle of nowhere.

Only problem was, this wasn't the first time she'd been here.

In this exact spot. Staring at another victim who'd been stripped bare and left to rot. Not just one. Three before now. Déjà vu grabbed hold and refused to let up, dragging her back three years, when she'd still been working for the FBI.

"Yeah. That's her." Ivy tried to swallow around the mass in her throat, but there wasn't going to be any relief here. Sweat gathered beneath her blazer, and her mouth dried. "Do we know anything about where she's been the past three days?"

Right on time. The killer she'd known had taken and held his hostages for three days before dumping them in strategic locations in the middle of the New Mexican desert. She and her partner had never been able to narrow down the location of their final moments. Though, looking back, she'd known this day was coming. That she would pay for letting a killer get away.

She just hadn't expected it to happen so soon. Or to one of her own.

"Nothing yet. The medical examiner is stuck in Albuquerque. Won't be able to retrieve the body for a couple more hours," Halsey said.

"She deserved better." A pressure she'd become familiar with over the course of the past two years bubbled behind her sternum. Purpose replaced the cold leaking of grief in her gut, and the distractions bled to the back of her mind. Ivy cataloged everything she could about the scene. No tire tracks. At least, none that they would be able to match to a specific make and model. The man who'd done this was careful, calculating. He'd gotten the best of her once upon a time, but she'd changed. She could be just as calculating when she had to be. "Grab some gloves. We need to turn her over."

Halsey seemed uneasy at the idea. There were rules in a crime scene. No one touched the body until the coroner or the medical examiner had a chance to do an external exam and document and photograph the victim, but they didn't have two hours to wait for the right authorities to get here. The relentless heat could be destroying evidence as they spoke. "Like I said, the ME won't be here for a couple hours."

"I know that. I'm asking you to break protocol." Ivy hated the manipulation lacing her voice, but there were times when it was all she could do to keep the bad guys from winning. "I need to see her back."

Halsey considered her a moment. He'd been involved with one of Ivy's operatives enough to get a read on her himself. That was one of the things she liked about the chief of police. Always asking questions, never satisfied with the answers. Eager to dig beneath the surface and find the truth. Whatever Halsey saw in her expression then had him convinced what she was asking was worth the risk of contaminating a crime scene. He pulled a set of latex gloves from his back pocket and shoved both hands inside before crouching beside the victim. "Looking for something particular?"

"I'll know it when I see it." Her breath seemed to double inside her chest, taking up too much space for her lungs to function properly. Nervous energy skittered up her spine as the chief gently rolled Dr. Piel onto her front.

And there it was.

The markings she'd decoded—too late—carved into the woman's back. Fresh. Jagged. Unrepentant.

"What the hell is that?" Halsey asked.

A bead of sweat escaped her hairline, dissolving her controlled appearance in an instant as the secure world she'd built around herself cracked wide open. "A message."

A shift rippled through the chief as the implications of her answer settled in. "A message. For who?"

She didn't have all the information yet. She could be getting ahead of herself, but instinct said this was the same man. The same killer. The one she'd fought to what she'd believed to be his death two years ago at the hand of her trusted pocketknife. Only to learn he'd escaped that dark basement when she'd recovered. There was something she had to do. "Take care of her, Halsey. I'll be in touch."

The chief repositioned the body as though they hadn't just broken the entire rule book of their investigative training manuals. "Where are you going? We need to coordinate so we can figure out where she's been the past few days."

"I need to make a call." Ivy forced herself to take

even steps in the direction of her SUV. To prove she could. That another body—a colleague—killed in the same manner as the victims from her last investigation for the FBI couldn't get to her. That she was as untouchable as she'd convinced herself she was when she'd built the most resourced security company in the world. But she was quickly learning that no amount of training or weapons, no amount of operatives and their K-9 units, could protect her from the failure clawing up her throat.

She locked herself inside her SUV, not even giving herself the chance to find relief from the heat. Halsey blocked most of her view of Dr. Piel through the windshield as he draped a tarp over the body. They couldn't risk the sun speeding up decomposition if they wanted an accurate assessment of time of death, but the woman's feet were still visible. This wasn't supposed to happen. She'd worked too hard and too long for the past to be able to reach her now. Ivy punched the vehicle's start button with her thumb, and the engine came alive.

This wasn't a onetime incident.

Her stomach rolled at the idea of another one of her operatives turning up dead. Jocelyn, Scarlett. But that wasn't the only way to hurt her either. While the killer preferred female victims over male, every one of her operatives had bound themselves to their significant others and partners in the past two years. They'd built their own families, one even welcoming their first child. If anything happened to any one of them…

Nausea churned hot and acidic as she pulled away from the scene. She'd built Socorro Security out of a need to protect those who couldn't protect themselves.

Those like the three women abandoned and killed for no other purpose than to draw Ivy and her partner in. Cartels like *Sangre por Sangre* fed off innocent lives, poisoned the very people they went out of their way to use, abducted children into their ranks and killed anyone in their way. But Socorro had put a stop to that. Ivy and her operatives had sacrificed and risked their lives for this. They'd made a difference. According to their inside source, upper management within the cartel had gone into hiding. The few remaining lieutenants were on the run. She'd done that. She'd saved lives.

And yet she hadn't been able to save one of her own.

Tears blurred her vision as she checked the rearview mirror. The crime scene was long behind her, but the weight of loss clung tight.

Dr. Nafessa Piel had been one of the first contractors Ivy had taken on. The work she and her operatives had engaged in came with casualties, mostly in the form of physical injury in the field. Bullet wounds, concussions, stab wounds. The cartels didn't fight fair, and they certainly didn't have any remorse for doing whatever it took to achieve their mission. Dr. Piel had been there right from the beginning. Ready to send contractors back into battle, a little more worn, but stronger.

Socorro Security was supposed to save the world.

Who was going to save its operatives now?

Ivy accelerated toward Albuquerque, letting the hour tick by without much thought. There was no point in heading back to headquarters now. She didn't have answers for the team, but from the soft ping of her cell phone every few minutes, that didn't stop them from trying to get them. She turned her entire focus on the mental map directing her to Fairview Memorial Park just as the air conditioner was beginning to penetrate through her slacks and blazer.

The cemetery wasn't large in any sense of the word, but it had been constructed in that unique Mexican-inspired architecture of sandstone monuments, bare patches of dirt and white grave markers. Light stuccos and black metal rods made up the columns standing guard over the souls forever resting inside. Ivy parked along the side of the road, gazing through the gate. She'd never come here before.

There hadn't been a need until now.

Ivy shut off her phone, disabling any kind of GPS. Though it wouldn't be hard for her security consultant to track her down if Scarlett put her mind to it. That was what Ivy paid her for. Only it hadn't saved Dr. Piel when they'd needed that skill the most, had it? Whoever'd killed their physician had known Socorro would find her. That had been his plan all along.

She shouldered out of the vehicle and rounded the hood. Slipping her hand into her blazer pocket, Ivy felt for the pocketknife she'd carried since leaving home at seventeen. The one that had saved her life when it mattered. She navigated through the gate and around the first few headstones. Once-pristine landscaping—dying grass, interestingly enough—spread out in front of her and made her search easier. A slope arched from her left, creating a slight hill with hundreds of markers, some a century old, staring back at her.

Seven from the right. Two back.

Ivy pulled the pocketknife and set it on top of the headstone of a name she'd never been able to forget. The third victim of her last investigation. The one that had led them straight to her killer. "It's time for us to finish this."

CARSON LANG WAS waiting for her.

Tucked into the corner of the apartment in one of the well-loved chairs. Out of sight. Clear line to the front door. Just in case he had to make a quick escape.

He hadn't bothered with the lights. Too exposed. Shadows hid the minute details of a woman who escaped here more than she wanted others to know. A knitting project—half-finished—splayed across the side table, her most recent read beneath it. This one a psychological thriller. Seemed she didn't get enough real-life mind games and danger in her work. She had to seek them out in fiction. It all added up to a woman who took charge of her circumstances. Who didn't wait for permission to take action or walk a straight line to get what she wanted, but there were softer sides to her, too. Ones she'd tried to hide her whole life. To prove she was worthy. That she wouldn't fail. That she'd climbed free of her past.

The scar directly over his right kidney testified to her softer side.

He didn't have to learn what kind of woman Ivy Bardot was by being in her personal space. He'd been watching her for a long time.

The front-door dead bolt flipped. The door cracked. Slower than he expected. Her outline maneuvered inside and closed the door behind her. Blocking his exit. A strong inhalation crossed the space between them. A distraction for him to focus on as she unholstered her sidearm.

She was good.

"Don't bother with the lights." He could practically feel the battle-ready tension ripple down her frame from here.

"It will look more suspicious if I keep them off." Her voice erased years of doubt, secrets and violence in a single sentence. Hell, he'd missed it. That connection to the outside world. A place where he'd once thrived with her at his side. "Not to mention it'll be harder to shoot you for breaking into one of my safe houses."

"You're the one who called me, remember?" He held up the pocketknife in front of the window to his right. Just enough light for her to register it. A piece of her he'd known had taken everything for her to leave on top of that gravestone and walk away.

Ivy set her bag on the entryway table beside the door, moving slower than he knew she wanted to go into the living room. Gun still in hand, she reached beneath the lampshade on the opposite end table. The entire space burst with brightness, and it took too long for his vision to adjust.

Except he couldn't take his eyes off her. Under the wrong circumstances the perps they'd apprehended had made that very same mistake, only for an entirely different reason. Her guard was up, based on the way she was scanning the rest of the apartment with those intense eyes that seemed to know far more than she let on at any given moment.

Something had changed.

Something had gone wrong.

She crossed the room and retrieved the pocketknife. As though she physically needed it in her possession. "I had no other choice. Where's my dog?"

Of course, that would be her most pressing question in this little exchange. It always was when they managed to debrief every few months.

"Max is downstairs in the SUV." The German shepherd had been a parting gift before he'd gone undercover. One that had ended up saving his life a couple of times. "Couldn't risk her drawing attention."

"Right." Ivy hadn't moved.

"What do you mean you had no other choice?" A heavy weight pinned him into his seat. Carson sat forward. This wasn't like her. Not the real her. Sure, she had to keep that legendary emotional armor in place when in the field and directing her team and Congress, but she didn't need to do that with him. They were partners. Didn't matter they were on two opposite ends of the spectrum at the moment. They would always be partners. "What happened?"

"One of my operatives is dead. Our physician." Ivy disappeared behind the wall separating the living room from the kitchen, her heels echoing through the safe house. Her direction changed, farther down the hall as she swept the rest of the place for threats.

He wouldn't take it personally. The things they'd seen as partners had nearly destroyed them. Any slipup, any mistake on their part, meant risking the very lives they were working to save.

"I'm sorry." Carson shoved to stand with every intention of pulling Ivy into his arms, but she wouldn't let herself slow down long enough for that to happen. Not now. "How?"

She slid back into his vision, holstering her weapon beneath the navy blue blazer that brought out the depth of emerald in her eyes. Ivy leaned into the wall, crossing her arms across her frame, and exhaustion caught up in her expression. "Did you know?"

"Know what?" he asked.

"That he was coming for me." There was a bite in her voice. Accusation. "Our last case together. When three women were found dead in the middle of the desert with symbols carved into their backs. We caught up with the killer. We barely made it out of that house alive. He got away through an escape hatch that led beneath the house and emptied out onto the back of the property."

"I remember the case, Ivy. The son of a bitch nearly killed you." Where was she going with this? Why had she pulled him out of the field? Why had she risked blowing his cover? To rehash an old investigation? "If it weren't for that case, we wouldn't have known about *Sangre por Sangre* until it was too late."

Sangre por Sangre. Blood for Blood. The cartel had clawed its way to the top of the food chain through brutality, abductions, underage recruitment, drugs and women. The organization demolished competitors and left nothing for police and the DEA to tie back to them. Socorro Security and Ivy's team of private military contractors had been the only ones to ever get close enough to bringing the cartel to its knees. With him feeding her the information she needed to do it. Now *Sangre por Sangre* was on the run. Desperate to keep itself alive. Carson was close to identifying the head of the cartel.

"He's been out there all this time, but no matter where I look, he's a ghost. We agreed you would go undercover in the cartel to find him. I quit the FBI because I didn't think the federal government could protect you as well as a private organization could, and I've kept my end of the deal. I built Socorro Security for you. You said you would find him, and we would end this. It's been two years, Carson, and we're as clueless as when we started." She slid away from the brace of the wall, standing on her own two feet when it looked as though she wanted nothing more than to collapse right here in the middle of the floor. "Who is he?"

"What is this?" She was so close, it wouldn't take much for him to reach out for her. But the distance she was purposefully putting between them set his nerves on edge. This wasn't the Ivy he'd gone undercover for. This was his former FBI partner, before they'd risked their lives for one another. Before he'd been injured in the field. Before she'd donated a piece of herself to save his life. And, damn it, he hadn't missed this version of her. He wanted more. He'd always wanted more for them. "Why the sudden interest in our last case? What is it you're not telling me?"

Ivy turned on her heel, heading for the bag she'd left at the front door. In seconds, she'd pulled something from inside and thrust it against his chest, every ounce the woman with the capability to bring the world to a stop with a snap of her fingers.

He grabbed for the paper crumpled under her grip. Not a piece of paper. A photo. Carson slipped it from her hand, instantly victim to the softness of her skin against his. The past two years had put him in a position of power, of respect, of camaraderie within the cartel. He was trusted by upper management. Though he'd never met the leader of *Sangre por Sangre*, Carson had proved himself time and again as a valuable asset. He'd made friends. Some of whom he'd fought beside as they'd taken their last breath in the field. Some who'd sat beside him in cuffs when an assignment went south. His fellow soldiers had been there for him. And, yeah, there'd been women. Cartel bunnies who were always more interested in what his position could give them rather than what he craved. But this… He'd missed this connection. The feel of Ivy. Her warmth. Her compassion. His heart rate ticked up at her mere touch.

Until his brain cleared enough to process the subject in the photo.

Dr. Nafessa Piel. Dead. Exposed. Left to decompose alone. Complete with added wounds carved into her back. Carson had seen this before. He'd lived it. Only it had been a different woman then. The symbols were different this time, too. This wasn't the same message the killer had left him and Ivy two years ago announcing *Sangre por Sangre*'s rise. "When did this happen?"

"The medical examiner hasn't been able to determine time of death yet," Ivy said. "But she'd been missing for three days."

"Same as the others. Let me guess—nothing but mucus in her stomach? Dehydrated, starved and tortured." The details would line up. She didn't have to respond. The answer was written all over her face. Carson forced himself to study every detail of the photo in an attempt to pick up on something they'd missed before. "And the message?"

"I pulled the old case file and compared these symbols to the ones left on the other three victims. He's evolving. Using a variation of the original, from what I can tell." The fight seemed to drain right out of her then. "I have a member on my team who may be able to speed up the decryption, but it's still going to take some time."

"Why now?" Carson offered the photo. "Why her?"

"Socorro has practically driven *Sangre por Sangre* underground, thanks to your intel and our manpower. This could be a final attempt to survive." Ivy stared down at the photo of her colleague, and a sadness Carson couldn't stand etched deep into her features. She would blame herself for this. And without hesitation she would take on the entire cartel to make it right. It was one of the things he admired most about her. It was why they'd gotten this far. She swiped her hand under her nose and grabbed for the photo. "As for why he targeted Dr. Piel, I was hoping you might have some insight."

He wanted to give it to her, but despite his years undercover, she knew everything he did about the cartel. "The last three victims betrayed the cartel. They were used as a warning to those who stepped out of—"

A red laser cut through the room between them.

"Get down!" Ivy lunged for him.

Just as a swarm of bullets exploded through the window.

Chapter Two

She was already reaching for her go bag.

Debris and glass rained down from above as the safe house's living room wall disintegrated under fire. Picture frames seemed to explode above her. Photos of happier times, of family she'd lost touch with years ago, of commendations from her career in the FBI. It was all being ripped to pieces by hot lead.

Ivy fisted the backpack she'd stashed beneath a section of the couch and kicked off her heels. Rolling off Carson, she dragged the go bag into her chest. The safe house she'd built to escape the day-to-day violence was falling apart around her, but she couldn't think about that right now. They had to get out of here. "Get to the bedroom!"

Whoever was on the other side of that gun would expect them to go for the door. But Ivy didn't like to follow expectations. Not even when it had come to taking the beatings her stepfather doled out on a regular basis when she'd been a child. Who would have thought a ten-year-old could shoot a man who was supposed to protect her? Based on his final expression, certainly not him.

Her partner was already moving. Carson shoved to

his feet, fingers encircling her arm. They moved as one, as though a single day and an entire war hadn't kept them apart for two years. He took the lead, surely already having mapped out this apartment. Leaving no chance for surprise.

Bullets punctured through the wall to their left. Every single one of them seemed to hike her nerves higher. Moonlight pierced through the holes left behind.

Ivy crawled on hands and knees down the hall right behind Carson. The bedroom was positioned at the end. Drywall and dust worked into her lungs, but she couldn't pay attention to the tightness in her chest right now. Sooner or later the gunfire would stop. The shooter on the other end would breach the apartment. They'd want to make sure they had hit their target. But she and Carson wouldn't be here. She had to make sure of that.

"Go, go, go!" The orders were unnecessary. What was he going to do? Stop in the middle of the hallway to have a chat? But the need to be in control, to feel as though she was doing something to get them out of here, had taken hold.

A single round ruptured through the wall in front of her face.

Ivy pulled up short as Carson turned back and locked his gaze on her, facing the reality the bullet could've dropped her right here and now. Too close. She forced herself to shake it off. They were going to die if they didn't pick up the pace.

Except the gunfire had stopped.

One second. Two. Longer.

No more shattering glass. No more close calls. No more attack.

They were out of time. "They're coming."

Carson lunged for the bedroom and somehow managed to land straight on her king-size bed.

She was right behind him, kicking the door shut. She threaded both arms through the backpack straps and secured it in place. Ivy unholstered her weapon and hit the release for the magazine. Fifteen rounds. Plus more in the go bag. They had a fighting chance.

"This is nice." Carson slid his hands over the comforter sprawled across the bed. "Much softer than that crappy mattress you had in your last place."

"It's one of those mail-order mattresses." She crossed to the corner window facing the next building over. It was one of the features she'd specifically required when she'd found this place. Corner apartment. Alley escape. Higher chances of getting out alive in case of an ambush. Most people didn't live that way. But she did. She had to. Unlocking the window, she pried the pane up and pushed the screen free. "No squeaky mattress springs. Memory foam. I sleep like the dead."

"Maybe one of these days I'll get to try it for myself." Carson was already on her heels as she maneuvered one leg through the window opening.

"Watch your step." She latched on to the overhead stucco ledge framing the window and tucked her toes into an identical one under her feet. The framing only extended the length of the window. They were going to have to make it to the railing on the floor directly beneath her. She'd practiced a handful of times, once scaring the crap out of Mrs. Orson, who'd taken to doing yoga outside, but Ivy wouldn't regret it now. "It's a long way down if you're not paying attention."

A hard thud registered from inside. Then another. The shooter was trying to breach the front door. It would take a while since she'd replaced the short screws holding the hinges in place with much heavier-duty ones. That, and she'd added a couple of dead bolts. It would take him at least—

The heavy door slammed into the wall behind it.

Not as long as she'd hoped. "Come on."

Stucco bit into her fingertips as she shuffled off to one side, out of line of the window, to make room for Carson on the ledge. He didn't waste time in joining her outside. These frames weren't meant to hold weight. They were purely decorative, and the longer they held on, the higher chance the construction would fail and they'd both die sooner than they'd planned.

Movement echoed through the apartment. Crunching glass. The shooter was on the hunt. For them.

Ivy steadied her breathing and turned her attention to the railing below. Ten feet down, five feet to the left. She hadn't jumped with the added weight of her go bag yet. She'd been building up to it in preparation for this exact scenario, but now she didn't have any other choice. They were going to have to risk it. She whistled low to catch Carson's attention, then nodded downward.

Disbelief and something along the lines of defiance spread across what little she could see of his expression. He shook his head.

All she could do was nod in response. A single word

could give away their position. She'd already lost Carson to the cartel once, and it had changed the entire course of her career and her life. She couldn't do it again. Ivy spread her weight evenly between both feet.

The movement inside the apartment was getting louder. Closer. They had a minute—maybe less. They had to do this now.

The weight of her backpack was beginning to wear on her. There was no encouraging Carson through facial expressions alone. She forced her attention to the target. Mrs. Orson's second-floor railing. Ivy redirected everything she had into her toes to give her the distance she needed. Her stomach vaulted into her chest as gravity took hold. The metal railing rushed up to meet her. Faster than she expected. Her fingers grazed the metal.

Then slipped.

She was free-falling. Every cell in her body screamed in warning.

Just as she clutched on to the bottom rail.

Her head hit the section of stucco holding up the second story. Her concentration frayed, and her hand lost some of its strength. Her legs swung out of control and twisted her body to one side. The ground seemed to move beneath her, threatening to swallow her up.

Metal reverberated through her a split second before a strong hand wrapped around her wrist and drew her gaze upward. Carson. He'd taken the leap. He was the only one keeping her from falling. His strength gave her enough direction to swing her legs back around. They still had another floor to go before they landed on solid ground, but right then it felt a little more possible with him watching her back.

Movement registered from her bedroom window.

"Watch out!" She pulled Carson over the railing as the gunman took aim. His weight intensified the pain in her shoulder and nearly dislodged her hold altogether. They had nowhere else to go. The first spray of bullets missed by a hair. The gun jammed, the click of an empty magazine echoing through the alleyway. Ivy had the feeling they wouldn't be so lucky the second time. The small muscles in her arm stretched longer than they were meant to. Any second now she'd drop him. "I can't hold on."

"Ivy, you have to let me go, or we're both going to die." Her partner seemed to gauge the distance between them and the ground.

Let him go? Had he lost his mind? No. She wasn't letting him go. She needed him alive. There was no way she could find Dr. Piel's killer without his insight into the cartel and the man she believed responsible for the murder.

The shooter slammed a new magazine into place and lowered the barrel of his assault rifle. At her. And yet Ivy couldn't seem to let her hand relax. Carson's weight was tearing her apart from the inside. She couldn't let him go. Not again. Not after everything they'd already survived together.

"You can do this. You have to do this, Ivy." Carson stared up at her, those dark eyes as familiar and foreign as she remembered. "I'll be fine."

She released his hand.

Carson hit the ground. At least twelve feet below. He landed hard enough for his legs to buckle, but then he was rolling out of the shooter's range. Ivy didn't hesitate. She released her own hold on the railing. The ground rushed up to meet her harder and faster than she expected. Her knees launched into her chest, but her backpack forced her to roll and redistribute the weight to save her from breaking her legs.

Asphalt exploded around her, and she forced herself to her feet. "Run!"

Only Carson wasn't there. He wasn't anywhere.

A high-pitched whistle from the end of the alley pierced her attention. Ivy pushed everything she had into pumping her legs. The gunman was three floors up. He would have a hell of a time intercepting them.

Unless he had a partner.

Drawing her weapon into her hand, she registered a cascade of police sirens in the distance as she rounded toward the front of the building. Mrs. Orson probably wasn't the only resident to call 911 at the sound of gunfire. Ivy just hoped no one had been hurt in the ambush. As much as she could leave the apartment and anything else connecting her to this life at the drop of a hat, the people in this building didn't have that luxury.

She caught up with Carson at the corner and followed him down the street to a black SUV stashed in one of the parallel alleys. Her vehicle wasn't an option. Whoever had targeted the safe house would already have her registration details, and if this was some kind of coordinated effort to hunt down and ambush Socorro operatives, none of them were safe.

"Get in." Carson climbed behind the wheel, with Ivy collapsing into the front passenger seat. Max made her presence known with a series of too-loud barks that could summon demons under the right circumstances, but apparently, Carson didn't have the heart to quiet her excitement for seeing Ivy. The engine growled to life at the touch of a button, and they sped onto the street. Keeping an eye on the rearview mirror, her partner relaxed over a series of seconds. "The life you built is over, Ivy. From here on out, we can only trust each other."

HIS HEART RATE hadn't come down yet.

Seemed no matter how many miles Carson put between them and Ivy's safe house, having his former partner here kept his entire nervous system on edge. Adrenaline had started to drain and left him feeling keyed up and exhausted at the same time. A dangerous combination when facing the possibility his cover had been blown. That he'd been followed. Or that someone had come for Ivy.

"Where are we going?" She stroked Max's fur with a soothing calmness that, at that moment, Carson wished she'd paid toward him, but two years was a long time. They'd kept in touch. Him slipping her cartel intel, her providing him the plan to dismantle *Sangre por Sangre* and the warning to steer clear of Socorro's next move. They worked well together in that respect, but in this case, time had made their wounds deeper. Not given them a chance to heal.

She didn't like not knowing every detail ahead of time, and she sure as hell didn't like not being in charge, but there were certain things he couldn't tell her just yet either. At least, not without him logically defending his use of cartel resources available to him, and he wasn't running on logic right now. "We'll be there soon enough."

"You're very good about avoiding having to answer questions," she said.

"How do you think I've been able to survive this long undercover?" He'd meant to lighten the mood. Because they both knew, out of the two of them, the FBI had chosen the wrong agent to send undercover within *Sangre por Sangre*. The only reason it hadn't been her was because of his skin color. His mother's Asian roots had made their mark around his eyes, but it was his father's Mexican heritage that defined him on the outside. That heritage had given him an entry point inside the cartel, but to survive its ranks, he'd learned the rest violently and strategically.

Ivy directed her attention out the passenger-side window but stayed physically connected to the dog they'd once shared as a couple. "Good point."

They'd gotten out of the city without incident, heading north, but it was only a matter of time before whoever'd come for Ivy scorched through the rest of her life as they had her safe house. Which meant her team could be at risk, too. And not just them. Anyone connected to Ivy. Operatives' families. Clients. Any family she might have left.

"The shooter was sporting an M4 assault rifle. Exclusively a military model with a high-capacity magazine. Not something you would normally find on the streets." Ivy's voice had taken on that tone she used for interviewing witnesses and suspects. Strangers. "Which makes me think Dr. Piel's murder and this ambush are tied back to the cartel. The timing would be a hell of a coincidence if they weren't."

He'd made the same connection. "She was your friend. The way you talk about her. It's not the same as when you've talked about your other operatives."

Ivy rolled her head back toward the center console. "It didn't start out that way. I hired Dr. Piel because she was the most qualified for the job. She was a general surgeon at Columbia University. The only female in the entire emergency department. I saw how hard she had to work just to prove she was meant to be there, while getting a fraction of the salary as others less qualified. Not just as a woman, but as a Black woman." There was that sadness again. A mere hint of the grief Ivy was most likely hiding from him. "She reminded me of...me. Of my time in the FBI. So I made her an offer on the spot. I convinced her to uproot her entire life to come to New Mexico. I provided her a surgical suite and clinic, paid her three times what she was worth and watched her do what she did best. Saving the lives of my operatives. Without her, Socorro wouldn't have been possible. I owe her a lot. Only I'm just now realizing I never took the chance to tell her that."

The SUV's headlights bounced as he turned onto an unpaved road cutting off the I-25. It wasn't well-worn like most others. Practically hidden in the expanse of the desert. Purposefully out of reach of wandering hitchhikers and curious civilians. Carson carved up the single-lane dirt path partially overgrown from lack of use. He couldn't remember the last time he'd been out here. Didn't know what was waiting for them at the other end either. "Did Dr. Piel talk about her personal life? Maybe a falling-out with friends, family, a neighbor?"

"No. Not that she mentioned." Ivy stared out the windshield, the lights from the console glimmering off the line of unshed tears in her eyes. His partner never cried. Not even when she'd believed she was about to die. Then again, a lot could change in two years. "And before you ask, I've already looked into her finances and phone records. She didn't have any money problems, and there wasn't any suspicious activity in her messages or calls. We drug test regularly due to the nature of our work and the missions we take on. Her results have never given me reason to believe she's anything more than the woman I believed her to be."

"Then we need to assume she was killed because of you. Because of your connection to her." Carson pulled the SUV in front of the safe house. Well, *safe house* was a bit modest of a description. This place was more like a compound. A base *Sangre por Sangre* upper management utilized in case of emergency. Only it hadn't been used much in the past six months for the simple fact there wasn't much management left, thanks to Ivy and her team. He switched off the engine but didn't move to get out. Not yet. "Ivy, we knew this would be a possibility going in. You've spearheaded Socorro's creation and this war against the cartel. You've rallied the entire United States government to back you without hesitation and put *Sangre por Sangre* in a position of battling for survival. Dr. Piel's death, the attack at the apartment... This is just the beginning. They will not stop until they've destroyed everything and everyone you love."

"What is this place?" Ivy leaned forward in her seat, taking in the expansive landscaping, architecture and driveway leading to a three-car garage off to the left. She didn't wait for an answer and shouldered out of the vehicle. Rounding to the front of the SUV, she turned on him as he climbed out of the driver's side with Max following suit. "Did you bring me to a cartel safe house?"

"It's the last place they'll look for you." He didn't know how else to explain his decision. In his head, bringing her here made sense. Whoever had come for her at the apartment was well resourced, had access to military hardware and was not afraid to hurt bystanders. This was the best option to keep her safe. Right under the cartel's nose.

"Or I'm walking right into their hands." Her concern was valid. For as long as he'd been embedded within *Sangre por Sangre*, there were still some things he'd been kept separate from. The head of the cartel's identity, for example.

"I would never knowingly put you in danger." Carson couldn't take this distance between them anymore. Not just physically, but emotionally. He might've been on assignment for two years, but he was still the same man she'd fallen in love with during their last assignment. They were supposed to be a team. Not...whatever this was. "You know that."

"Do I?" Her jaw set hard enough to cut glass, but there was still an edge of nervousness. As though she expected to have to make a run for it at any second. "Because it was easy to contact you those first few months, Carson, but you stopped contacting me altogether. After a while, I was the one arranging our meetings. I was the one having to pull intel out of you instead of you offering it. That wasn't how this was supposed to work, or did you forget that while killing anyone the cartel pointed you at?"

Tension bled into every muscle along his spine. Every shot, every kill, had been ingrained into his head. There was no way he'd ever be able to forget the voices that had begged for their lives. No way he could ever forgive himself for the futures he'd stolen in the name of *Sangre por Sangre*. No matter their level of evil. But her accusation that he'd forgotten his purpose in all of this—that he'd defected into the enemy's ranks—gutted him. "I couldn't blow my cover. Every time I reached out increased the chances of exposing our operation and putting your life in danger. We knew what we were getting into when the special agent in charge approached us with this assignment, Ivy. You're the one who stepped away from the FBI's support and took it upon yourself to compartmentalize who was involved. You agreed to all of this."

"I thought you were dead. Do you know what that feels like? To believe that your partner can't get word to you that he's in danger? That you're helpless to do anything about it?" Ivy swiped at her face. She lost the battle of facing off with him, escaping back to the SUV. Except she didn't stop at the SUV. She kept walking. Heading toward the main road.

Carson didn't have an answer for her. Not the kind that would make her feel any better when exhaustion, adrenaline and anger were working to undermine her executive function. He trailed after her, keeping his distance. For now. "Where are you going?"

"I'm not just going to hide out in some cartel safe house and wait for the son of a bitch who killed my operative and came after me to make his next move. I need to know if the rest of my team is in danger." She pulled a phone from her blazer pocket. The screen lit up around her as she pressed her phone to her ear. "I can have an extraction here in twenty minutes."

Carson grabbed the phone from her hand. He tossed it on the ground and stomped it into the dirt with the heel of his boot. The metal and glass protested, but he couldn't risk broadcasting their position. "Whoever killed Dr. Piel wasn't responsible for what went down at the safe house tonight."

"You needed to destroy my burner to tell me that?" She seemed to come back into herself, the anger bleeding from her expression. "How can you be sure they're two separate incidents?"

Max whined between them as the tension thickened.

"Because the killer we're looking for prefers a blade. He likes to get close to his victims and make examples out of them. A gun is too messy. Traceable through ballistics." Any second now, he'd lose what little trust was left between him and Ivy. He couldn't let that happen. He couldn't lose her, too. "My guess? The ambush was a distraction. Something shiny for us to chase. And if I'm right, that means whoever killed Dr. Piel is already using it to his advantage."

Chapter Three

She felt as though she needed to wash off the evil.

It seemed to seep in from the walls, the floors, the top-of-the-line appliances and pretty tile. The bedding calling to her very sleep-neglected brain. She wouldn't touch any of it. This entire compound had been bought with the blood of thousands of innocent lives. Lives she'd sworn to keep safe from the cartel. Most she'd been too late to save.

Carson must've come here before. During his assignment.

Their conversation wouldn't stop replaying in her head. She'd accused him of losing perspective over the course of this assignment. She'd practically called him out as a cartel soldier who mindlessly followed his next order, and she hated herself for it. But worse, she hated her admission of how much she'd worried about him while he'd been undercover. Feelings weren't her strong suit. They'd done nothing but betray her and had been used against her in the past. And some habits died hard.

"Hungry?" He was the only one who could breach her personal space without triggering her defenses. Carson offered her a bowl-like plate of something orange and creamy with beans. "Cannellini beans with garlic, cherry tomatoes and onions."

"You just happen to have all the ingredients for my favorite comfort meal on hand?" She couldn't resist the promise of food or the fact that he'd taken the time and consideration to cook for her after what they'd been through tonight. Was it tonight? She wasn't sure how long ago a gunman had ripped apart the life she'd built separate of her crusade.

He withdrew the plate a couple of inches. "Is this your way of saying thank-you?"

A tendril of shame heated in her cheeks, and she took the plate. She was boxing him in as a potential threat when Carson had done nothing but fight beside her in the limited time they'd been thrust together. "Thank you."

The heat felt good in her hand. Grounding and strong. Or maybe it had nothing to do with the plate and everything to do with the partner handing it to her. A partner she'd missed more than anything. Ivy took her time with the first bite, letting the combination of garlic and onion soothe her down to her very bones.

Carson backed off, giving her space in a seemingly endless expanse of emptiness surrounding them. "Better?"

"Much." Calories had a way of making everything better, but she'd never gotten over his cooking. No matter how many times she'd tried re-creating the recipes in the old recipe book his mother had put together for him when he'd gone off to college, it wasn't the same.

"Still think I've been brainwashed by the cartel?" he asked.

The soup lost its taste, and suddenly she wasn't as hungry as she'd thought. "You've been invested in learning everything you can about *Sangre por Sangre* for the past two years. You've done things for them. Gotten to know the men and women that make up their ranks. Is it so hard to believe you may have started coming around to their way of thinking?"

"Going so far as to serve you up on a silver platter?" He was right there. No longer concerned with her need for personal space. The heat of his body drove through her T-shirt and soothed the aches of hitting the railing.

Ivy directed her gaze to the plate of food in her hand. He knew her better than anyone else in the world—inside and out—and there was a part of her that wanted to convince herself he would use that information against her. Only that part was lying to her. "We've been fighting this virus for so long, sometimes I start seeing threats where they don't exist."

Carson slipped his index finger under her chin and notched her gaze higher to meet his. "I'm not the threat, Ivy. Not for you. Ever."

Her nerves frayed under his touch, and she was instantly lost in the feel of him. Of having him this close. How long had they starved themselves of moments like this? How long had they let the job rule how they interacted with one another? Pretended their mission was more important than their feelings for one another?

Too long.

She was the one to maneuver the food he'd made from between them. The plate missed the edge of the kitchen island and fell. Glass exploded from the impact, spreading far and wide with the soup across the tile. She didn't care. Neither of them cared as she rose onto her toes and crushed her mouth to his. Ivy arched into him, pressing against him in an attempt to make them one, and the hollowness she'd suffered without him these past two years waned. In seconds, she was breathless. He did that to her. Had from the beginning.

It didn't matter that they'd been partners, that the FBI had put rules in place to keep agents from getting romantically involved. There'd always been a loyalty from Carson she couldn't ignore. Not just to the job. To her. In a lifetime of always looking for the best way to survive, for once, she'd felt as though she had someone at her back. And, damn it, he felt so good.

"I've missed you." Her words vanished into his mouth. In his arms, she wasn't the head of the Pentagon's only weapon against *Sangre por Sangre.* She wasn't calling the shots or grieving the loss of one of her best operatives, and with that came a sense of freedom. Of unburdening. It had been so long since she'd given herself permission to drop the weight of responsibility at her feet. But Carson made it easy to be herself. Safe.

"I missed you, too." He moved his hand over her rib cage—right where she needed him—but pain spiked into her chest and down her hip.

She sucked in a hiss of air, pulling back, as she grabbed her side. Lightning streaked across her vision. Ivy tried to swallow the nausea climbing up her throat, but there was no stopping it as long as her ribs were screaming for relief.

"You're hurt." Carson didn't waste time waiting for her

to deny it. Dropping behind the island, he pulled a first aid kit from underneath one of the cabinets.

"It's nothing. Just a bruise." Reality was rushing back. Too fast. She wasn't ready to let go of the past few minutes. Because she wasn't sure how much longer it would be until they allowed themselves to drop the roles they'd taken on again. "Is there a bathroom in this place?"

He stood there. Waiting. Waiting for her to let him help her. To be the one who burst into the room and fixed everything, as he had during their last case together. But the truth was, they weren't those people anymore. Time and violence and death had contorted them into something hard and unrecognizable. "Yeah. Down the hall. Second door on the right."

"Excuse me." Ivy wouldn't question his confidence. He'd been here before. In this place. In what capacity, she didn't know, but he was obviously more familiar with the cartel's setup than he'd reported.

She memorized the layout as she moved into the hallway, catching an office first. Cleaned out. What were the chances *Sangre por Sangre* had left something behind for her to use against them? What resources had they been forced to give up when the last few remaining lieutenants had gone underground? Her fingers itched to find out, but the pain in her side hadn't subsided.

She bypassed the bathroom as her legs threatened to collapse right out from under her. Adrenaline had run out within minutes of the ambush. She hadn't eaten anything other than that single bite of dinner in close to twenty-four hours as she'd tried to piece Dr. Piel's movements together from the past few days. Her go bag was stocked with food and water, but she'd left it back in the living room. As much as she hated to admit it, a piece of her needed the distance from Carson. To work this out. To put things back in perspective.

Ivy leveraged her hand against the wall as she moved down the too-long corridor. Room after room, stripped, abandoned. Papers discarded, shredders overflowing. Until she found one room furnished with an actual bed. The pressure of keeping it together popped before she managed to close the door behind her. Big breaths did nothing to counter the hurt pressing into her from all sides. Her nervous system was processing Dr. Piel's murder, the ambush at the apartment, the reunion with the man who'd promised her forever, the kiss they'd shared. The reminder a killer had slipped out of her reach. It was trying to bring her back to neutral, but there was just so much stuff in the way. She barely had time to take in the setup of the rest of the room before hiding away under the covers.

Cutting off her senses was the only proven method of bringing her out of a tailspin. It had been a long time since she'd felt this…powerless. But the past few days had compounded until she wasn't sure she was strong enough to take her next breath. At least, not anytime soon.

A low moan registered through the heavy comforter a split second before the mattress bounced with additional weight. A wet nose prodded underneath the seam of the blanket until Max had fully made her way inside the barrier between Ivy and the rest of the world.

"You always seem to know when you're needed." She wrapped one arm around the German shepherd, giving in to the warmth and the weight of the symbol of the relationship she and Carson had once created together. It all seemed so broken now. Foreign and strange. The longer Ivy stroked Max's fur, the sooner the pressure subsided, until she almost felt like herself. Almost. There were still a few pieces missing and unsure, but Max made the edges less sharp.

If she was being honest with herself, Carson had, too. He'd helped get her out of the apartment. Protected her when the gunman had taken aim. He'd risked his life to ensure she kept hers. That hadn't changed in the years they'd been apart.

But as sleep dragged her into unconsciousness, a single thought followed her under. One Ivy hated to consider at all but would be reckless to ignore.

That despite the attack on the safe house tonight, Carson was still utilizing cartel resources. And she wasn't sure she could trust him anymore.

She and Max had fallen asleep together.

Carson couldn't tear himself away from the sight as the past superimposed over the present. Of Ivy surprising him with the pup once he'd been released from the hospital at the end of their last case. Of the sheer look of joy on her face, so different from the woman he'd come to know as a partner. No longer burdened. But free. They'd been through hell together. Nearly died for one another. He'd lost one of his kidneys in the process. The kidney his mother had donated to keep him alive when he'd gotten sick a few years ago, but Ivy had done something unthinkable at the time.

His partner had given him one of her own.

She'd saved his life in more ways than one.

It was a miracle their blood types had matched. Her work with the FBI and her crippling terror of becoming victim to any kind of vulnerability had kept her healthy and strong, and when the time had come, she'd been there for him when it'd mattered most. Had brought them closer together than ever. But something had changed.

Ever since he'd accepted this assignment.

These past two years had separated them physically— he couldn't deny the shift—but what he hadn't expected was the emotional fallout keeping them apart now. The fallout that made him feel like he'd made up everything between them up to this point.

This job, the one he'd taken to find the killer they'd let slip away, had been their only chance to cut *Sangre por Sangre* off at the knees, and they'd done a hell of a job together. The cartel was dying off. What else could he do but finish what they'd started together as a thank-you for everything Ivy had sacrificed for this cause?

The transplant scar—doubled in thickness now— prickled with awareness as Carson watched the slow rise and fall of Ivy's shoulders. Secret exchanges of information, coded messages, slipped documents—they were nothing compared to being with Ivy in person. Feeling her pressed against him, hearing her breathing change as he got close. He'd taken a risk going to that apartment last night. Now, faced with the possibility his cover within *Sangre por Sangre* had been blown, Ivy was all he had left.

A stab of regret cut through him. Rising through the cartel's ranks hadn't been a singular event or a solitary one. The men and women—the soldiers—he'd fought beside had become friends in a sense. People who considered him one of their own. He'd laughed with them, mourned with them, fought with them. Most of them were dead now, but there were a few who'd gone to ground. If he wanted to find the bastard who'd killed Dr. Piel and the three women before her, he'd need their help.

"It's rude to stare." Ivy shifted on the bed, careful not to wake Max. They'd both learned early on how illogical a German shepherd could be when ripped out of her beauty sleep, and they'd paid for it several times in the way of torn clothing and chewed shoes. Neither of them could risk it at this point. The clothes they were wearing were all they had for now. But all Carson could do right then was admire the sunrise coming through the window framing Ivy's face. "How long were you going to let me sleep?"

"As long as you needed," he said. "Figured you could use the rest before we decide where to go from here."

"And by here, you mean using a cartel property as a safe house." The severity in her expression had drained in sleep, leaving a hint of the woman he remembered before they'd gotten themselves in this mess.

Coming here might not have been the best choice, but they'd made it through the night. He probably wouldn't have been able to say the same for a Socorro property.

Sangre por Sangre had learned the locations of each and every hideout Ivy's operatives utilized. Carson didn't know where upper management had gotten the intel, but he hadn't been willing to risk putting her in more danger. Not when he'd just gotten her back. Keeping her here—close—was his only option. "Not going to let me live that one down anytime soon, are you?"

"No." She maneuvered out of bed with nothing short of grace despite her constrictive clothing and the sidearm holstered beneath her blazer. Her blouse had earned a few more wrinkles, almost making her human. She let her hand sweep down Max's back. "I can't believe how big she's gotten. I remember bringing her home the night you came home from the hospital. Neither of us could even get off the couch after the surgeries, but she didn't seem to mind. She just wanted to be held, and we all ended up asleep in the living room of your tiny apartment."

A warmth he'd convinced himself he'd been cut off from a long time ago prodded at his chest. That night had changed everything. Given him a small glimpse of the future he'd do anything to have. With Ivy. Little did either of them know it would be one of their last together. "A lot can change in two years."

"Yeah." She seemed to come back to the moment right then. Stiffening. Treating him as though he were a stranger despite her very blood coursing through his veins. "Does this place have coffee?"

"Already brewing." Carson dipped for the duffel bag at his feet. He tossed it Ivy's way. She caught it, but he hadn't expected anything less.

"I'm going to get cleaned up. I think there's still glass in my bra." His former partner disappeared into the attached bathroom. Within seconds, the sound of water hitting tile emerged underneath the door, with a thin veil of steam escaping with it.

It would be easy to cross this room, to open that door and reclaim what they had. He'd strip her free of that makeshift armor she presented to the world and join Ivy underneath the water. He'd memorize her body— her taste—all over again and remind himself what he'd been fighting for all this time.

But he wouldn't.

Max stretched across the bed, rolling to her back. The German shepherd was still half-asleep. As though these four walls could protect them from what was coming. Carson knew better. There was no escaping the cartel. Least of all for him. And he wasn't going to take Ivy down with him.

He peeled himself away from the bedroom door and forced himself down the hall. Mere weeks had passed since the last time he'd holed up in this compound. Upper management had given him the responsibility of recovering a large fentanyl shipment moved from one of their distribution warehouses during a Socorro raid. Scarlett Beam and her DEA partner had torn the place apart in an attempt to recover the boy *Sangre por Sangre* had abducted to force the DEA agent's compliance. Billions of dollars in fentanyl had simply disappeared into thin air. No trace. No witnesses. No profit for the cartel.

Carson had made sure of it.

Though a handful of soldiers had paid the price. People he'd gotten to know in this very compound. Through late nights. Rounds of beers. War stories. Family regrets. A hook had caught in him. One that refused to let go. No one else could see it. No one else understood. He'd been tasked to walk a line between two competing worlds, and his loyalties had split over the course of this assignment. His heart and soul had been committed to ending the cartel's evil influence on innocents, to stopping the destruction they'd caused from the very beginning. But living among *Sangre por Sangre* had shown him there were innocents caught on both sides. Family members of soldiers, even some soldiers themselves whose loyalty had been based on fear more than respect. He couldn't abandon them. Now one of those worlds was on the brink of destruction. What was he supposed to do then?

Carson shoved the memories to the back of his mind as far as they would go at the sound of movement from the hallway. Max's nails ticked off the tile as she searched for breakfast. "What'll it be today?"

She gazed up at him with those big black eyes that had seen too much in their short amount of time together. More than a companion should see.

"All right. Pancakes it is." They were Ivy's favorite, and since he'd taken the liberty of stocking this place back when he'd been working for the cartel, he was sure they had the ingredients to do it. Carson went through the pantry cupboards surrounding the refrigerator. "Any opinions on toppings?"

"I'm partial to raspberries." Her voice struck him

harder than he expected. As though his entire nervous system had been waiting for a hit of her. Stepping into his peripheral vision, Ivy scrunched a towel into her hair, the ends of which contrasted with her light skin tone across her shoulders and collarbone. She took a seat on the other side of the island. "But I'll take anything other than a granola bar at this point."

His breath seemed to catch in his throat. The black tank top and cargo pants weren't anything special, but they weren't Ivy. Not the FBI agent and security CEO he'd come to know. The woman across the kitchen from him was the one he'd gotten to know behind closed doors. In the privacy of their homes as they'd figured out how to become more than professionals. More than partners. And he couldn't help but stare. "You clean up nice."

"It's amazing what a toothbrush and a shower can do, isn't it?" She tossed the towel onto the back of the other bar stool. "There was talk of coffee."

"Help yourself." He motioned to the mugs and pot on the counter to his right as he grabbed for the base pancake ingredients. "Sorry to disappoint, but there aren't any raspberries."

"I'm not hard to please when it comes to food." Ivy maneuvered into the kitchen—close enough for him to feel the leftover heat of her shower—and filled two mugs with straight black coffee. The way he'd come to like it given the cartel didn't spring for sugar and creamer on most jobs. Handing one of the mugs off to him, she seemed to melt at her first sip. "Hunger is the worst feeling in the world. I'll do whatever it takes to avoid it most days."

He couldn't help but laugh at the memories of the few times they'd been caught in the middle of a stakeout without something to eat. He'd never seen a more perfect example of Dr. Jekyll and Mr. Hyde in those moments. To the point he'd started packing snacks in his vehicle. For her. "I remember."

A softness filtered across her expression then. "Everything seemed so much easier back then. We took orders, we did our jobs and we went home at night. There wasn't this...nervousness that followed us around."

"What do you have to be nervous about?" Making pancakes slipped off his priority list, much to Max's annoyance as she poked her nose into the side of his leg. But all Carson had attention for was Ivy. For this sudden introspection she seemed to fall into. "You and I are more than equipped to handle anything that comes our way. We've proved that a dozen times during our time with the FBI alone."

"You mean apart from the possibility the cartel could come through those doors at any second and kill us both?" Ivy wrapped both hands around her mug as though it were some kind of life vest. "This feels different."

"Because we don't have the resources of the FBI behind us?" he asked. "Or because you think Dr. Piel might've been involved with *Sangre por Sangre*?"

Chapter Four

"That's not possible." She hadn't wanted to say the words out loud, but the dark temptation was there. It came from her investigative training, the same training that had helped her connect the dots between three dead women in the desert and their killer.

The idea one of her operatives could be involved with the very cartel responsible for most of the holes Dr. Piel treated made her sick to her stomach. But there was a pattern. The man who'd strangled and murdered those women and then left their bodies in the desert for her to find two years ago had done so as a warning. To encourage those who attempted to leave *Sangre por Sangre* to reconsider.

There's no escaping Sangre por Sangre.

The message carved into those women's backs hadn't been clear from the beginning. Their killer had used an encryption that had taken too long for Ivy to solve. Not to mention decomposition, swelling and the heat had warped the carvings in their skin. That case had nearly cost Ivy her life in the process. Had Dr. Piel gotten caught in the cartel's web? Two years was a long time. The son of a bitch responsible could've come at

Ivy at any point during that time. Had good reason to as she and her operatives had chipped away at the killer's layer of protection. *Sangre por Sangre* didn't extend their protection services for nothing. The killer would have to have already been a member. Or given the cartel something they'd wanted.

In the end, it didn't matter. She'd made a promise to those women. She was going to finish this. And she wasn't going to let a drug cartel get in the way.

"As much as I hate to think someone in the cartel got that close to you, you and I both know it's a possibility, Ivy. But something must've changed. Dr. Piel must've tried to get out. This could be the killer's way of punishing her like he did with those other women." Carson always seemed to be able to read her. Better than anyone else. It was the small considerations that showed how fiercely he committed to others. How intensely he loved the people in his life. His mother before she'd died, Max, her. Equally, that intensity could turn him into the worst enemy if given enough heat. "Do you have any reason to believe Dr. Piel might've needed the cartel for something? Does she have a relative in their ranks?"

Acid surged into her throat, and Ivy suddenly didn't have a taste for coffee anymore. She set the mug on the counter, nerves raw. "No. Like I said, her financials and phone records don't indicate any contact with anyone on the cartel's roster. But we both know once you ask the cartel for help, you're theirs forever."

Goose bumps prickled down her arms, and in that moment, she'd never felt more naked despite her clothing. A tank top and jeans were logical in case they needed to make a quick escape, but her blazer and slacks had served her well in the past. With her uniform— brought into her security life from her time in the FBI— nothing was impossible. She could command armies, raise funding for missions, train K-9s and protect her team. But now...there was no clear path here. No agenda she could pinpoint, and that left her exposed in a way she'd avoided since she was ten years old. "In truth, I think I'd rather this be about me. At least I would have something to aim at."

"It's still a possibility, especially considering the attack at the apartment, but as long as we're work- ing blind, you're going to have to avoid everything and everyone you know." Carson got to work mixing whatever ingredients he'd pulled from the pantry in a metal bowl. He knew exactly where everything was in this kitchen, and the realization hurt more than she expected. He was comfortable here. In a compound owned and operated by the very people tearing their cities apart, people they'd vowed to bring to justice. Just how deep had he committed himself to their cause during his assignment? "That means Socorro hideouts and resources."

Her gut hollowed. The comparison wasn't lost on her right then either. How the killer they were hunting had hidden behind an impenetrable wall of cartel protection while she'd built her own layer of armor with Socorro. Without her team and resources, they wouldn't survive. The cartel would find them here. Maybe not tonight. Maybe not tomorrow. But soon. Every single cartel safe house she and her team had raided came with security measures patched into a mainframe that fed back to an undisclosed location. There might not be many members of *Sangre por Sangre* left, but security would be a priority. Someone would figure out this compound wasn't empty. "You're asking me to trust you with my life."

Carson's grip on the whisk tightened, but his rhythmic mixing didn't even falter. "You've done it before. Is it so hard to believe you can trust me now?"

She didn't know how to answer that. What he wanted from her. At the start of this, she wouldn't have hesitated, but now? Her partner was right. A lot changed in two years. "You've been chasing this killer since you've gone undercover, Carson. All that time, you've supplied me and the Pentagon with information on cartel shipments, safe houses, lieutenants, soldiers and plans. Complete with names and photos of every soldier. Invaluable information that has brought the cartel to its knees." She regretted putting her mug down so quickly, leaving her empty-handed and cold. "But every time I asked for intel on the man who killed those women, you haven't been able to supply anything useful. No photos. No names. No ranking. According to your reports, he's a ghost. At first, we thought he might be a lieutenant, but they're all dead now. There's the possibility he's one of their contracted killers, but his MO hasn't turned up anywhere else in the country, according to Alpine Valley PD."

A knot of tension built between her shoulder blades. She watched him. For a change in his expression. For something to tell her she was wrong. "I was willing to believe your theory he's a lowly soldier for a while, but what are the chances you wouldn't have come into contact with him all this time? Which makes me think maybe you did find him. And there's some reason you're not telling me. So, yes, Carson, it's hard for me to trust you with my life right now. Because I'm not sure I know who you are anymore."

"And bringing you here?" Carson ceased his mixing then, turning to face her. "Risking my cover to help you escape your apartment last night? You think I would do that just to hand Socorro's founder over to upper management on a silver platter?"

"I don't know why you brought me here. Other than you've obviously been here before. You know where everything is. You knew what was stocked in the pantry, that this place would be empty." Her lips dried the longer she scrambled to put the pieces of the past twelve hours together. "Or maybe that was all part of the plan to gain my trust. So you could feed me whatever reason you have for lying to me all this time."

He backed out of the kitchen as though she'd physically assaulted him. His voice lost the confidence she'd always felt from him. "You saved my life, Ivy. I have one of your organs keeping me alive. You've known me for years. We were partners. We had each other's backs. Do you really think I could just hand you over to the people who want you dead like that?"

"Then tell me who he is." She couldn't help but counter his retreat, closing the distance between them. "Give me something to go off of, something I can use to make him pay for what he's done."

"I don't have what you want, Ivy. I've handed over every piece of intel I've uncovered while on assignment within *Sangre por Sangre*." He wasn't trying to escape anymore. He'd taken a stand. "What I can tell you is that there hasn't been a single day I haven't regretted going undercover within the cartel or leaving you to fight this battle on the outside alone. I knew what I was getting into, but I sure as hell never expected my own partner to question my loyalties."

She didn't know what to say to that, what to think. He was right. She'd been the one attacking *Sangre por Sangre* from the outside, taking the credit, making the big moves to dismantle the cartel while he'd been forced to keep to the shadows, to give up everything he'd known and cared about. Carson had never been one for glory. It wasn't in his nature, even as a rookie agent closing his first case. And he deserved a hell of a lot better from her. "I'm sorry. I think I've been at this for so long now, I'm constantly on the lookout for the next threat, and without one staring me in the face, I maybe started creating one where there wasn't any danger."

"I know exactly what you mean." He reached for her then—as though she hadn't just accused him of betraying her, their cause and their country—and pulled her against his chest.

Right where she needed to be. She didn't like being caged, but in his arms, the thud of his heart took off the edge. It was a rare occurrence for her to relax with anyone else around, a gift from the chaotic and abusive childhood she'd endured for so long. But Carson had been the first person she'd given herself permission to trust. Because he'd earned it. "I just want this to end. I want everything to go back to the way it was."

"There's no going back, though, is there? Not for us," he said.

"No. I suppose you're right." They'd left everything they'd known as a couple behind when he'd gone under-cover. Left the FBI, left their homes, left their part-nership. They'd set out to create something new—to do something good in the world. And this...this was new territory for them both, a crash of two worlds that didn't quite fit together. Ivy deadened the anxiety of not knowing what came next with a deep inhalation, pulling away. Pulling herself together. "Which means the only way out of this is *through.*"

"Where do you suggest we start?" he asked. "The killer we're looking for is really good at staying under the radar."

"Then we work backward," she said. "We start with figuring out if Dr. Piel was involved with *Sangre por Sangre.*"

ALPINE VALLEY PD had cordoned off the property, but from the look of the seal on the front door, the official search hadn't been conducted yet.

Dr. Nafessa Piel's single-level home sat back away from the road with a dozen other cookie-cutter houses lining both sides of the street. Hardscaping had been maintained—no stone outliers on the driveway or pavers waiting to trip some kid on the sidewalk—in a simple design with sections of different rock to create move-ment across the flat stretch of land. From what Carson understood of the victim, extravagance had never been one of Dr. Piel's values, mostly noted in the lack of polish on the woman's nails and a single item of simple gold jewelry in the crime scene photos Ivy had shown him. He expected nothing but that same conviction inside.

Ivy pulled her pocketknife from her jeans and slid the blade along the sticker sealing off the home from nosy neighbors and murder groupies. She hesitated just before pushing inside, glancing back at him. In that moment he was thrust back into the partnership they'd each given up for this cause. One where she took the lead and he could do nothing but follow. Only that couldn't be the case anymore. They had to do this together. "All of our operatives are supplied with a security system when they sign on with Socorro. The alarm will trigger the second we open the door if Alpine PD hasn't already disabled the system. I could put a call in to my security expert, but if you insist on not using Socorro resources, I'll have to enter the override code manually."

The alarm could alert the neighborhood and the police to them breaking a threshold they had no business crossing during an active homicide investigation. But the punishment for giving *Sangre por Sangre* any kind of lead on Ivy's location was far worse. "Then we make this quick."

"All right. I've been here a few times since the installation. The panel is in the entryway, on the right wall." Ivy tested the doorknob, and it turned easily in her hand. She pushed inside.

But there was no sound of the alarm.

Shadow stretched out in front of them, and Carson's nerves rocketed into overdrive. Every cell in his body wanted to maneuver Ivy behind him, to protect her from any threat that came their way, but doing so would deepen the cracks in their partnership. She'd trained with the best, employed the best and worked tirelessly to become the best. That hadn't changed.

"The police department must've already disabled the alarm." She unholstered her sidearm. FBI agents and officers alike knew without a doubt house calls were the most dangerous part of the job. No telling what waited for them on the inside of a home. Or if a homeowner had set a trap to avoid containment. Her boots echoed off ugly tan tile lining a vaulted entryway, common in New Mexico houses.

Carson closed the door behind them.

The entryway dumped them into a front room furnished with leather couches, a mounted TV, a coffee table and an expansive rug to absorb the cold chill shooting down Carson's spine. Light filtered in through the back of the house from the kitchen, currently out of sight. "You said you've been here before. Anything different from your last visit?"

The admission hadn't meant much to him on the other side of the door, but he saw the relevance now. Ivy had been here several times, enough to know where the security panel was located and the basic layout of the home, past the fact her company had installed it. Which meant she and the latest victim had more than a professional relationship. They'd been friends. And not in the way a boss protected and interacted with her employees. There was a heaviness in the way she moved. As though expecting Dr. Piel to greet her with a smile and announce this had all been a misunderstanding. Why wouldn't Ivy have told him of their personal connection from the beginning?

"No. Everything looks the same, as far as I can tell." Ivy motioned to her right, down a length of hallway that angled into a different section of the house, as she took the left.

The place was much larger than he'd originally estimated, with multiple bedrooms and bathrooms. It was a lot for an unmarried woman who lived alone and spent most of her days patching up a team of private military contractors. He kicked at the base of the first door branching off the hallway and took aim inside. Empty. Gray carpet—new, from what he could tell—stretched out beneath a queen-size bed made up for guests. Another TV had been mounted on the wall. Nothing in the closet. No attached bathroom or signs of recent use.

Carson forced himself to move on. There was something off about this place. Why the hell had their victim bought such a large property? He searched the next bedroom, then an office and the primary bedroom. Everything in order. Everything in its place. No backups of lotion or conditioner or cleaning products. Personal photos and memorabilia were sparse and primarily in the largest bedroom. It was as though this place didn't really serve as a home.

More like a safe house.

Tension ratcheted into Carson's shoulders with every second he was separated from Ivy. Holstering his weapon, he retraced his steps until he located her going through drawers in the kitchen. "This place has four bedrooms."

"I know. No bugs or surveillance, from what I can tell, though." Ivy closed one of the drawers and moved on to another. "I would tell you this place was for friends and family that stayed frequently, but from what Nafessa has told me about her past, she didn't have anyone close, and she didn't like to host. She mostly kept to herself. Talked very little of her life outside of Socorro. It took months working with her before she let the smallest detail slide."

There were pieces of this puzzle that were starting to line up, but Carson didn't want to bring those into her awareness. Pieces he couldn't prove. Yet. "That's the first time you called Dr. Piel by her first name. Why didn't you tell me you two were closer than her as a contracted employee with Socorro?"

"Because there's honestly not that much to tell. She lived alone. Kept to herself. Whatever was between us was…new, in a way. Just within the past few months." Ivy abandoned her search of the kitchen. "It started as greeting each other in the halls, to sitting at the dining table during lunch."

"Who instigated conversation?" he asked.

"I don't remember." A healthy dose of suspicion tainted her voice, and right then, it felt as though the years hadn't torn them apart.

This was what they were good at. This was what they did best. Working off each other, testing theories, testing statements. He'd missed that. More than he thought he had.

Carson memorized the decor and personal touches, which didn't take long. Everything seemed to have a sense of order. Everything in its place. Or at least that was what the victim had wanted them to believe. That someone lived here. That this place was nothing more than a cookie-cutter home that served as a refuge to a private security physician. He moved into the living room, picking out more details. The lack of wear or imprints on the couch. The dust settling over the bookshelves. Adults played victim to their habits. A favorite spot on the couch while watching TV, a stack of books on an end table, even a preferred burner on the stove. But from what he could tell from this place, Dr. Piel didn't have any. "Did she ever ask about you personally?"

"Of course. That's what people do when they're becoming friends." Confusion deepened the lines etched between Ivy's eyebrows, but it didn't last long. She was never one to let an emotion—any kind of emotion—linger longer than necessary. She'd never seen a reason to. "If you're worried I gave away your undercover identity, you can relax. Nobody in my office but my counterterrorism agent Granger Morais knows that information. He figured it out a few weeks ago, and he isn't the type to spread the news."

"And what did Dr. Piel tell you about herself in return?" Every relationship in existence—biological, romantic, created—was transactional. Give and take. There were rules to follow and expectations to meet.

"She came to New Mexico from Columbia University when I offered her the contract. General surgery. Before that, her background was in emergency medicine at an array of different hospitals." Ivy folded her arms over her chest as she settled back against the kitchen counter. "She was an only child to a single mom. Her mom passed away when she was a teenager. Drug overdose. She put herself through school and went to medical school on scholarships."

"Did you speak with her references before you offered her the contract with Socorro?" He pulled the couch cushions up, one by one. No crumbs. No loose change. Nothing to suggest this couch had been here more than a few days. Hell, he could still smell the plastic covering it had most likely been delivered in.

"Of course I did. She came highly recommended from each of her supervisors, especially at Columbia." The defensiveness he'd come to expect played around her eyes and straightened her shoulders.

"Who reached out first?" he asked. "When you were looking for a physician, was she the one to make the initial contact?"

"Yes. I put the word out I was looking for a physician through my contacts in the Pentagon. She was one of the first who submitted her CV, and I made an on-site visit to Columbia." Ivy rounded into the dining room, just within his peripheral vision. "What are you doing?"

"Has this couch always been here?" There was a fire burning beneath his skin now, feeding into a theory he couldn't ignore anymore. "The times you visited, was this the same couch that was here?"

"What?" A realization seemed to spark in her eyes. "No. I…I spilled wine on the cushion last time I was here. She must've replaced the couch."

"Why not just have the cushion cleaned or replace that single piece?" Instinct drove him to throw each cushion out of the way. "Why replace the whole couch?"

"What the hell does a couch have to do with anything?" There was a bite in her words that hadn't been there before. A raw nerve he'd touched. "The woman's body is decomposing in the refrigerator of Alpine Valley's only emergency clinic with strangulation marks around her neck and knife wounds in her back, and you want to focus on the fact she bought a new couch?"

"Yes, because I don't think Dr. Piel bought it. It smells too new." He shoved the couch free from its position in the living room. And found exactly what he was looking for. "And I don't think she pays the mortgage on this place or actually lives here."

"What are you saying?" She couldn't seem to keep herself away, coming closer. "Is that...?"

"Blood." Carson fought to keep his breathing steady as he studied the brownish-red spread that hadn't come clean from the tile's grout. He couldn't help but lock his gaze on hers. "It's likely Dr. Piel was killed right here."

Chapter Five

Alpine Valley PD had taken control of the scene. She hadn't had any other choice but to notify them since this had likely been the location of Dr. Piel's death.

The other women they'd recovered in the desert, the three who'd lost their lives on her last case for the FBI, had been killed in and around their homes. This case seemed to be hitting the same markers.

"What were you and Mr....?" Chief Halsey left the question open, a pen raised over the notebook in his hand, but she wouldn't finish that sentence for him. Carson Lang no longer existed. Her partner had become Dominic Rojas, a *Sangre por Sangre* cartel soldier with a rap sheet longer than the US Constitution, and there was no way in hell she'd take the chance of compromising his cover by putting his name on paper. If she hadn't compromised it already.

"What do you think we were doing, Baker?" She hadn't meant the words to sound so harsh. Baker Halsey had gone above and beyond to overcome his resistance to accept and collaborate, but it had taken falling for one of Ivy's operatives to bring him around. "Nafessa Piel was one of my employees, and now she's dead. Did you really think I was going to sit back while your department investigated her murder?"

"I was hoping you would pay me the same respect to do my damn job as I give you and your team, and I seem to remember sealing this door so as not to disturb a potential crime scene. From the look of it, the seal was cut through. Most likely with a blade." Intense blue eyes the shade of a clear sky centered on her, but Ivy wasn't the type to fall for a pretty face or drawn-out silences. She'd faced down senators and military officers. She'd built a security company from the ground up when it became clear the federal government couldn't protect Carson on the inside of a cartel. Chief Halsey had a job to do, but she'd learned police tactics a long time ago. They wouldn't work now. The notebook disappeared into his uniform jacket pocket. "Any idea how that happened?"

Red and blue patrol lights swept across her face from the chief's vehicle parked in the driveway, almost hypnotizing. The events of the past hour raced through her head. Cutting through the seal, searching the house. Finding evidence of blood beneath the couch. Carson's accusations replayed on repeat, no matter how many times she tried to override them.

That Nafessa Piel had targeted Ivy and Socorro. That the physician had worked her way into Ivy's confidence with patience, probing questions and expertise. That the house they were standing in right now hadn't been a home, but a safe house.

No. She wasn't entertaining this idea. It was crazy.

Okay. Yes, Dr. Piel had been the one to reach out to

apply for the position. Yes, she'd been the one who'd initiated her and Ivy's friendship. She'd been the one to take that first step and invite Ivy over for drinks, and Ivy had said yes. Because the thought of going another two years without direct contact from her partner had made the black hole in her chest so much worse, and having a friend—someone she could connect with— had felt important.

Ivy's mouth dried as she was forced back into the moment. "No. I don't know how the seal on the door was broken."

"I see. And what about him?" Alpine Valley's finest was smarter than that. Chief Halsey nodded toward Carson, standing with a deputy she didn't know on the other side of the room, but there was something along the lines of humor playing in the corners of Halsey's mouth. "There a good reason the founder of Socorro Security has partnered with a cartel soldier on your little rogue expedition?"

Panic infused the muscles down her spine. Ivy breathed through her initial response to deny the truth. "I don't know what you're talking—"

"That man saved my and Jocelyn's lives," he said.

The intensity she'd noted a few minutes ago drained from around the chief's eyes.

"To be honest, I still don't know why," Halsey said. "We were in their territory, fair and square. I was ready to tear their entire building down to get Jocelyn out alive when he walked in with six armed cartel soldiers. He took one look at Jocelyn, and it was like he knew her. Like they'd been friends for years."

She let his assumptions hang between them.

"He's one of yours, isn't he? Planted in *Sangre por Sangre*'s ranks." She hadn't given Chief Halsey nearly enough credit in their short time working together. The man had definitely earned that badge and the title of Alpine Valley's hero. He directed his attention to the living room. "Too bad I got here after the people who'd broken into this property had already gone. Didn't get a chance to get their statements. Sure was lucky I discovered the bloodstain beneath the couch, though."

His meaning took a moment to sink in.

"Yeah. Lucky." She detached herself from the gravitational pull the chief seemed to exude by taking a single step back.

"One more thing, Ms. Bardot." The chief pointed the end of his pen at her. "Heard about what went down at your apartment. Jocelyn has been calling me nonstop since the news broke. I'm guessing there's a reason you're not in touch. All this have something to do with keeping them in the dark?"

"I'm not sure yet, but I have a feeling it won't be long before I find out." Nervous energy played at the tips of her fingers. The longer she and Carson stayed in one place, the more attention they were bound to garner from the wrong people. But she couldn't leave until she got what she came here for. "Has the ME finished the autopsy on Nafessa Piel's body?"

Halsey lowered his voice, coming in a few inches closer. "I took your advice and reached out to your old special agent in charge for the file on your last case. The FBI isn't usually so agreeable, but once I mentioned your name, he was all too willing to cooperate. I read through your notes and passed them on to the medical examiner. Three women left in the desert, strangled, with messages carved into their backs. Despite the variation in the characters recovered on Nafessa Piel's back, the ME has ample reason to conclude this latest murder fits the MO of the killer you were chasing back then. He's willing to state there's a connection between both cases."

Confirmation. Her stomach knotted tighter. She'd been willing to make the leap based off unproven facts, but there was no denying the truth now. The man they'd let escape two years ago was killing again.

"Watch yourself, Ivy. I've seen firsthand the lengths the cartel will go to to get what they want, and I know you have, too." A sadness she couldn't begin to understand creased in his jaw. "I've got this covered. Whatever it is you're after, I trust you know when to bring me in."

"There is something I need you to check for me." Dread pooled at the base of her spine, but she hadn't built her career without considering all the options. No matter how hard it was to swallow. "I need to know if Nafessa Piel has an off-the-books connection to *Sangre por Sangre*. No matter how small. Anything they could've used to manipulate her. Quietly, please."

"Those other women's deaths you investigated, you theorized they were all trying to get out of the cartel's grip, and that's why they were targeted. To send a message to deserters." The chief's gaze bounced around the house, as though the walls were listening. "You think that's the case here?"

"I'll be in touch." She nodded thanks. Carson followed her out of the house. It wasn't until they'd pulled away from Dr. Piel's home that she had the guts to break the silence between them. "It's him, Carson. The medical examiner confirmed a connection between Dr. Piel's murder and the case we worked back then."

"We're going to find him." Confidence resonated in every word. He reached across the center console and took her hand in his. Warmth spread up her arm from the contact and chased back the chill that had taken hold from searching that cold, empty house. "He's going to pay for what he's done, and we're going to finish this. Together. I give you my word."

His reassurance was enough to ease her denial of Dr. Piel's involvement in her own demise. For now. They'd potentially uncovered the scene where Socorro's physician had been killed, but there were still so many questions they didn't have answers to. And Ivy wasn't sure she wanted those answers. She stared out the passenger-side window as the houses in the neighborhood ticked by, begging her mind to switch off. To forget the outline of a pool of blood stained into the tile of her friend's home. Her only point of grounding contact was the hand still in hers. "Is it hard for you to be undercover?"

He didn't answer for a few breaths. "In some aspects. Not so much in others." She'd resigned to not getting more than that from him, but Carson went on. "There were things I missed at first. My own bed being one of them. I was never alone. The lieutenants exerted power any chance they got with orders and privileges. Metias Leyva—the lieutenant your forward observer went up against to protect Leyva's ex-wife—was probably the worst. Our meals were cold and few and far between.

We mostly slept on cots or the ground or in the back seat of our vehicles. We're tools to be used. Nothing more."

Everything he'd described stabbed deeper than she expected. The conditions he'd suffered would've broken any man, but Carson had held on. For this assignment, for their agreement to not let the *Sangre por Sangre* virus spread. She studied their interconnected hands resting on the center console. That was one of the things she'd loved about him. His loyalty. His commitment. No matter how much risk came with his decision, he'd always been one to stick through it. "What aspects weren't so hard?"

"There were things that made taking orders easier. Knowing why I was there, knowing our end goal, helped. After a while, I started to get to know some of the other recruits. Some of us got…close." He brought the back of her hand to his mouth, planting a kiss there. "Most of all, I guess the thing that made everything not so bad was knowing, sooner or later, I was coming home to you."

A battle ensued within. Warning spiked in her gut at his mention of the other cartel recruits with such… fondness, countered with the warmth of his simple assurance. But Ivy couldn't trust her instincts right now. Carson's theory concerning Dr. Piel—that one of her own people might've been involved with the cartel she'd taken an oath to dismantle—was starting to make sense.

Ivy directed her attention out the window. And started planning her next move.

CARSON HAD GONE through the crime scene photos a dozen times.

Nothing had changed.

The FBI had done nothing more to find the man responsible for three women's deaths once Carson had agreed to go undercover within *Sangre por Sangre*. The case had been abandoned on their end. No new evidence. No witnesses coming forward. It was as though the federal government had simply given up. The victims' bodies had been released to their families, the evidence cataloged and filed away in some storage locker that would take an act of the director himself to release.

Exhaustion blurred the reports in front of him. They'd come back to the cartel safe house to regroup, but they were getting nowhere. No matter which way they looked at it, they were right back at square one. Just as they had been before he'd gone undercover. The medical examiner was in possession of the most recent body. There was little chance he and Ivy would be allowed anywhere near it, and he couldn't risk taking the chance the cartel already had eyes on Dr. Piel's remains. All he and his partner knew was there was a solid connection. The man who'd killed those victims two years ago had come after a Socorro physician. But why now? After all this time, the son of a bitch Carson had been hunting had lain low in the cartel's ranks. Was this about Dr. Piel? Or was this about Ivy?

"Anything new?" Her voice had lost its assertiveness in the past couple of hours. Draining with every dead end they came across.

He pushed back away from the kitchen island. Crime scene photos, initial reports, his own handwritten notes from another lifetime ago covered every inch of the quartz surface. None of it had done him a damn bit of good. "I've been through everything. Twice. The house we cornered the killer in two years ago has since been sold and bought by an elderly couple with clean background checks, and the two soldiers I fought that night trying to get to you in time are still serving time in prison."

He scrubbed at his face. How long had it been since he'd slept? Twenty-four hours? More? He couldn't tell anymore. Adrenaline reserves had run out a long time ago, and the pancakes they'd had this morning had already been spent. This was the part of the assignment he hated the most. The dead end. Serving the drug cartel had been simpler, in a way. He'd taken orders and carried them out. There'd been bullets occasionally, but for the most part, he'd been secure in knowing he wasn't the one responsible for any kind of loss of life. Not like he had been with the FBI.

"I've been through every piece of paper the cartel left behind in this safe house. There's nothing here." Ivy moved in close, directly over his shoulder, and invigorated his senses with a hint of vanilla and soap. It was enough to keep him from spiraling in the moment, but the effect would wear off the more he starved himself of sleep and calories. "What about the intel you gathered within the cartel? Anything that might give us a lead? You said you got close to some of the other recruits. Maybe one of them mentioned someone within the organization that liked to strangle his victims before carving messages into their backs?"

She was fishing for information, and hell, Carson didn't blame her. It was in Ivy's nature to have a plan worked out in her head before she took the next step, but a defensiveness that had no business coming between them surged. The people he'd gotten to know within the cartel's ranks had been sources. Nothing more. And yet there was a part of him that needed to protect them as much as they'd protected him since he'd joined their ranks. "I've kept records of everyone I came into contact with since the moment I joined *Sangre por Sangre*, but the people I worked with were foot soldiers. Grunts who didn't know anything. It was the lieutenants that issued the orders. The founder of the cartel kept his identity in the dark by making us go through them."

His mind went straight to the one man who'd gotten him through most of the assignments that'd left his hands covered in too much blood. Sebastian Aguado had been with the cartel nearly his entire life. Saved Carson's life on more than one occasion. And was rewarded for that loyalty with the loss of his wife and children—violently—after a rival cartel had abducted and killed them in retaliation. *Sangre por Sangre* hadn't done anything to stop the slaughter. Leaving Sebastian with nothing. There was a chance his old friend might want to even the playing field by helping him and Ivy root out the head of the cartel. Hell, he might be the only resource they could rely on.

Ivy's exhalation brushed the back of his neck. Too close. Too familiar. Too dangerous at a time like this. Because the moment he took his eyes off the end goal, the cartel would strike. He couldn't risk making any mistakes. Not when it came to Ivy.

She shifted her weight away from him, as though

sensing his need for space. "And from what you've reported…"

"They're all dead. Socorro made sure of that." He hadn't meant the statement to take the shape of an accusation, but there it was. They were in an impossible situation. One he didn't know how to fix.

Other memories, of Carson having to step up and be the man of the house when his father had left him and his mother high and dry, surged forward. He hadn't been able to fix anything for his mother either. It didn't matter how good the grades he earned were or how much money he contributed to their expenses when he was old enough to get a job—he couldn't fix other people's mistakes. And now the one person he had left in this world—the one person he trusted—was caught in the result of his own failure. There'd been a time when all Carson wanted was to do something good with the second chance he'd been given after his mother had donated a kidney to save his life. Then again when he'd lost that kidney in a fight for Ivy's life and taken on one of hers. But this… Nothing concerning this case gave him hope this could end in anything but misery. "I'm going to get some fresh air."

Ivy didn't respond as he shoved away from the kitchen island and headed for the back door. He clocked the cameras positioned at the exit, but he'd ensured the cameras installed around the perimeter of the property had been taken off-line weeks ago.

Carson wrenched the sliding back door open with a bit too much force, earning himself a bark from Max. She followed him out the door beneath the covered porch. New Mexico had a peculiar habit of being too hot and too cold at the same time. Or maybe it was just his brain playing tricks on him as he stared into nothing but a fenced yard of dirt and weeds in the middle of January. Every piece of evidence, every witness statement, every lead jumbled through his mind. Out of order, upside down.

Despite years of undercover work—of following orders, of taking out every target required, of watching his fellow soldiers bleed out beside him and giving up everything he'd known in the process—he was nowhere near closing in on the killer who'd nearly taken Ivy from him. Who'd killed those women.

His phone weighed heavy in his pants pocket. There was still one option left. Sebastian had been able to avoid being buried six feet under with the rest of the cartel. Within the past month, whatever remained of *Sangre por Sangre* had scattered, "every man for himself" style, and his mentor had been no exception. Carson had heard whisperings the lifelong soldier in his fifties had fled back to his hometown of Aztec, but they'd just been rumors.

Carson forced himself to take his next breath slower than he wanted. Reaching out to anyone in the cartel directly—even with his cover intact—could unleash a hell neither he nor Ivy was prepared to deal with. Not to mention it could give Ivy reason to distance herself from him even further.

But what other choice did they have at this point?

Ivy had been targeted. Not just at her apartment, but possibly by a sociopath sending her a direct message by taking out one of her employees, and there was no way he would sit back and lose her. Not again. They'd fought too hard and for too long to let someone else have a say in their future. Least of all a killer. His fingers tingled with the need to send that message. He checked over his shoulder. For Ivy. But she must've remained in the kitchen. Most likely to go through the files they'd built over the past two hours. Carson unpocketed his phone.

Max locked her gaze on him, cocking her head to one side. In judgment.

"You want to go home, don't you? You want to go back to sleeping in a bed with your mom instead of on the ground with me?" He was more than aware of the ridiculousness of expecting his K-9 to answer back. He was also cognizant of how he was projecting onto his partner his own internal motivations for even considering contacting a man who'd dedicated his entire life to *Sangre por Sangre*. But Sebastian had roots deep into the organization. Twenty years' worth of experience, loyalty and know-how pertaining to all cartel business. Carson had heard the stories—the legend—of the soldier who had single-handedly undermined the DEA investigators over the years. Didn't hurt that Sebastian owed him a favor.

The German shepherd licked one side of her mouth.

"That's what I thought." He tapped out the message one-handed and hit Send. "Time to pay up, old man."

The back door protested on dirty tracks, centering Ivy over the threshold. "Thought I might join you for that fresh air."

Carson slipped his phone back into his pocket, just out of her line of sight. "I've had worse company."

"You're talking about Max, right?" A smile cracked at the corner of her mouth. Something private and meant only for him. It was her tendency to only reveal bits and pieces of herself to people she trusted that had first gotten his attention in the FBI. Why he'd requested to become her partner despite his lack of experience and the fact she'd driven most of her previous partners into early retirement. He'd wanted to be one of the few she trusted. Considering their partnership had dipped into a personal relationship, Carson would say he'd succeeded. Until she determined otherwise. Ivy crossed the porch to the railing at the edge of the cement, fingers interlaced as she searched the backyard. He'd never seen anything more beautiful in his life, never seen something more worth fighting for than her. "It's peaceful out here. I can see why you like it."

He joined her at the railing. "First time I came here, I was part of a security detail for a lieutenant named Tolenado. Turned out I had the most experience of anyone else on the team. Tolenado noticed. Decided to bring me on as one of his enforcers."

His pocket vibrated with an incoming message. Sebastian's response.

"I remember Tolenado. He abducted and tortured a war correspondent for three days. Intended to kill her, too. Right up until my operative Jones Driscoll pulled her out." She seemed to memorize the layout of the land spanning behind the house. "That correspondent was the one who broke the news a state senator had allowed

Sangre por Sangre to kill ten US military soldiers to undermine Socorro. He failed, though."

"That's because you believe in what you're doing out there," Carson said. "From the very beginning, you were willing to do whatever it took to protect the people who couldn't protect themselves. Including me. I like to think that conviction has rubbed off on me."

"Except I couldn't help Nafessa or those other women from getting killed." Her voice hooked into him. "I went back through the intel you've gathered over the past two years along with the locations of the cartel's safe houses and the names of every *Sangre por Sangre* operative you encountered. At this point, we're treading water with no land in sight."

Carson pulled his phone to his side and read Sebastian's message. The old man had come through. "Then we start swimming. Right into the belly of the beast."

Chapter Six

Turned out the belly of the beast Carson had mentioned took the form of a small town she'd never heard of. Aztec, New Mexico, stood as home to an array of natural arches, forgotten ruins and six thousand people at the very top of the state. The town itself sat so close to the border between New Mexico and Colorado, they could practically cross state lines within minutes. Was that why *Sangre por Sangre* had chosen this location? Or was there anything here at all?

She studied the grid-like design of every street, the homes surrounded by dead lawns and bare earth. Cement driveways had cracked over time, giving up the ghost to overgrown scrub brush and cacti. There was an expansive difference between Albuquerque and towns such as Aztec. While big-box stores and skyscrapers moved in to mask cultural origins and wipe slates clean, places like this went out of their way to protect tradition and the history of their people. She could see it in the architecture. Not forced or inauthentic but preserved. "What makes you think the cartel has any resources here?"

"Rumor has it one of the cartel's top soldiers survived Socorro's purge. From what I've learned about him in the past, he considers Aztec a safe haven. Someplace no one will come looking for him." Carson kept his gaze on the road ahead. "I haven't been able to verify the intel. Honestly, I'm not sure there's anything for us here, but I figured if we were going to get any information on Dr. Piel's killer, this could be our best shot."

A lead. Her stomach fluttered, and for a reason unknown to Ivy, she wanted nothing more in that moment than to unholster her sidearm. "And if this cartel soldier doesn't want to share what he knows?"

"That's why we brought Max. She has a way of making people talk." He flashed her a smile meant to extinguish the nerves funneling through her chest, but Ivy felt nothing but apprehension at the idea they were walking into a *Sangre por Sangre* trap. "There's an entire arsenal in the cargo area, too."

"Who is this guy? And why hasn't he come up before?" The more information she had, the better decision she could make. That was the way this worked. Learning about this lead two days into their investigation didn't sit right. Though there wasn't a single bone in her body that believed Carson would put her in the cartel's crosshairs on purpose. Up to this point, he'd gone out of his way to ensure her safety. Hadn't he?

"Sebastian was my recruiter when I first joined the cartel. He watched over me, brought me into his circle. Trained me." There were emotions in those few statements Carson tried to bury, but she'd become an expert at reading him in their partnership. Something wasn't right here. There was something he wasn't telling her.

"I saved his ass during one of Socorro's last raids on *Sangre por Sangre*'s headquarters a few weeks ago. Your counterterrorism agent Granger and his partner brought the entire place down on itself by taking out the underground tunnels the cartel was using to continue operations. I kept Sebastian from becoming one of the casualties."

"So he owes you his life." Why didn't that fact make her feel any better? "And you think an active member of *Sangre por Sangre* would be willing to turn on the cartel?"

"Sebastian has only one priority—survival. Whoever provides him the ability to do that the best is his friend. And at this point, Ivy, he's our only chance. No one but the lieutenants and the founder themselves have been with the cartel as long as this guy," he said. "If the killer we're looking for is active again, Sebastian can tell us who he is. For a price."

She wedged her boots into the floor as Carson maneuvered the SUV onto a barren street along the north edge of town. A beaten sign that was too difficult to read this time of night swung from rusted-out chains with a short burst of wind ahead. "I'll have to trust you on that."

He slowed his approach as oversize metal gates materialized through the darkness. A motion sensor–activated spotlight beamed to life, shining directly through the windshield.

Ivy brought her hand up to block the assault. Blind to any threat that might be waiting for them in the darkness.

"We're here." Carson shoved the SUV into Park and

switched off the ignition. Max maneuvered her head between the front seats as though in an attempt to get the lay of the land before having to exit the safety of the vehicle.

Ivy felt the need to do the same, but the spotlight had yet to relent. She shouldered free of the SUV, her boots sinking into softened dirt. The gates stood as sentinels keeping unwanted visitors out, but the open structure and years of wear allowed her to see past the form-fitted plastic blocking most of her view inside. "Sebastian No-Last-Name lives in a junkyard?"

"A place like this comes with a lot of benefits. It's off the grid, you have to deal with very few visitors and there's access to a variety of vehicles in case of emergency." Carson rounded the head of the vehicle, the SUV's headlights exposing every strained vein in his forearms. No matter how much he trusted his own intel, there was obviously still a good amount of unknown he hadn't accepted.

Ivy joined him in front of the gate, responding in a singsong rhythm. "And there's plenty of places to hide a body or two."

Max huffed between them. Almost desperate to get this over with. The pressure growing heavier in Ivy's chest agreed. The sooner they could get out of this dark, rotting hellhole, the better. Preferably alive. The main building spread out to her left. She clocked two single roll-up doors and an expansive warehouse built from white metal sheeting. No vehicles parked in front. Aboveground power lines cut across the single-lane road they'd taken to get here and disappeared into the dark.

This place was isolated. Far from prying eyes. And much larger than any auto recycling operation she'd come across before. "I hope this isn't a mistake."

He raised his gaze to the corner of the gate. "Smile for the camera, Ms. Dixon."

Dixon. She hadn't used that alias in years. Which meant Carson didn't trust Sebastian with her real identity. Why?

Her curiosity got the best of her, and Ivy directed her attention to the surveillance camera mounted overhead. The gate snapped open without being touched, and Carson pushed inside. Remote locks. The spotlight died out the moment she followed after, leaving white spots across her vision. Disorientation acted as an operative's best friend, and whoever the hell was inside knew it.

Ivy itched to unholster her weapon, but a move like that would put both her and Carson in danger before they'd gotten the information they needed. She followed her partner's lead, Max trailing a few steps behind. Only a few dimmed lights punctured into the overhang of the main building lit their way. Multiple rows of cars—every make and model—had been arranged in rows as far as the eye could see, and she couldn't help but wonder if *Sangre por Sangre* had utilized their pick of illegal VINs over the years. Perhaps switched out a few license plates. "I hope you know what you're doing, Rojas."

The back of the property rose into somewhat of a hill and showcased additional vehicles parked facing toward them, adding strain to her already-tight muscles.

"That's far enough, Rojas," a voice said from the

shadows clinging to the warehouse. "You know the drill. Weapons, please."

Carson slowed, then pulled to a stop at a side door to the building. Unholstering his sidearm, he spread his arms wide before tossing the weapon a few feet ahead of them. "I come in peace."

"Does she?" a voice asked from the dark.

An invisible pool of dread leaked into her gut. There was no way in hell she was giving up her weapon. Not to a man tied to the very organization who'd killed innocent people for profit and domination.

Putting her in his sights, Carson nodded at her sidearm. "He won't talk to us unless we're unarmed."

"Then I guess this was all a waste of time." Ivy searched the darkness for a shape, an outline, for any evidence they weren't walking straight into a cartel ambush. One hand on the butt of her weapon. The weight of Carson's gaze remained on her in expectation, but she wouldn't budge. Not for the slim chance of getting what they came for. There had to be another way.

Carson lowered his arms, turning to face her. In an instant, he'd closed the distance between them, each footstep punctuated with the groan of wet gravel and dirt. He slipped his palm over the back of her hand set against her sidearm. "For Dr. Piel."

Three words. That was all it took for her to release her hold. To give up her only protection. Because the truth was Ivy owed Nafessa Piel whatever it took to bring her killer to justice. Months of conversations, of shared meals, of invites into personal spaces. Thousands of texts and emails. For the first time—possibly since she'd been ten years old—she'd had a friend. Someone who wasn't scared of her murderous past or holding a personal agenda. It didn't matter Socorro's physician might have had a connection to the cartel. Ivy didn't care. This killer—the man who'd targeted four women—used those victims as a warning to those wanting to leave the cartel behind. Which meant it was possible Nafessa wanted to leave the cartel behind. She'd wanted out.

Ivy's hands shook as Carson drew her weapon from her shoulder holster, tossing it beside his before turning back to the owner of that mysterious voice. Disorientation. Vulnerability. These were the attributes of someone who liked to be in power. In control. But Ivy wouldn't give in.

"That's better." Movement registered near the building, but the moon's light wasn't strong enough to reach into those dark places, leaving Ivy blind. "Now, to what do I owe this visit from my old friend?"

As though Carson Lang had never existed, Dominic Rojas took shape in her partner's features. Harder, more intimidating, stronger. The kind of man who used that strength to overpower others. It was an impossible— almost supernatural—shift that left her cold. "I'm calling in my debt, Sebastian."

"I see." Gravel crunched beneath heavy footsteps as Sebastian moved to the edge between light and dark. Though Ivy still couldn't see his face, the gun aimed at her and Carson was perfectly clear. "In that case, come on in."

"Te voy a matar." I'll kill you for this. His Spanish had gone rusty in the years he'd chosen to speak his mother's

language of origin, but the message was perfectly clear. Sebastian would pay for this. Every defense Carson owned shot into the forefront of his mind as he raised his hands, palms forward. He maneuvered in front of Ivy. "We had a deal."

Max growled low in her throat, ready for the command to strike, and Carson was almost ready to give it.

"And yet you brought Socorro's CEO straight to my door, *mi amigo*. Did you honestly believe I wouldn't recognize the woman responsible for *Sangre por Sangre*'s destruction?" Sebastian kept his face in shadow, using the warehouse behind him as an added layer of protection. "Because of her, our brothers and sisters are six feet underground."

He had a decision to make, a split-second reaction that would either get him and Ivy killed or give her a chance to walk away. Carson turned on Ivy, advancing with every pound he had on her. "Is that so? You told me your name was Christine Dixon, and you sure as hell didn't say anything about being involved with Socorro Security."

Ivy notched her chin higher, but there wasn't an ounce of confusion in her expression. She was good at this. Had trained him well in their too-short time together as partners. "Would you have brought me here if I had?"

He reached for her. Secured a hand around her neck and pulled her into his chest. Not in the least bit hurting her. It was all for show. A way for them to get out of this alive together. Her hands latched around his wrists, her thumb directly over the thinnest section of skin. His pulse skyrocketed as he tried to find a way to get her out of here. "I don't like being lied to."

Carson cut his gaze toward the back of the property, where the lights from the warehouse didn't reach so easily. She was going to have to run.

"I'll send you an apology card." Her shoulders tensed. A split second before she rammed her knee into the top of his thigh.

Pain lightninged down his leg, but it was nothing compared to the real thing of taking a strike to the groin. He released his hold on her neck and hit the ground. Ivy took off, kicking up gravel and wet dirt behind her.

A gunshot exploded from behind as Sebastian attempted to stop her from escaping. The bullet ricocheted off the nearest vehicle with a spark. Missing his partner.

Max shifted on all four legs. Her bark echoed off the cars surrounding them as Carson got his bearings. The junkyard stretched several acres in each direction. With any number of hiding places. She just had to disappear until he could neutralize the threat himself. *"Pass auf!"* Sebastian didn't speak German. There was no way he'd be able to understand the command for Max to protect Ivy.

The K-9 bolted straight ahead and into the dark. She would do whatever it took to keep Ivy safe. "Split up. She can't get far without a weapon," he said to Sebastian.

In reality, Ivy's survival training had readied her to thrive in the worst circumstances. It was her way of protecting herself, of being prepared for any situation and coming out on top, and she'd ensured each and every single one of her operatives could do the same. Including Dr. Piel.

"You find her, bring her to me. She's mine. Understand? Those Socorro sons of bitches are going to pay for what they've done." Sebastian split off to the left as Carson followed after Max.

"We'll see about that." His boots suctioned into soggy dirt as the land failed to soak up the last of the winter rainstorms. The ground had acclimated to extreme dryness over the decades. A single storm could wash out roads, flood towns and trigger mudslides without warning.

He shouldn't have brought her here. Ivy was out here, forced into a position of self-defense because of him, but there was no point in shaming himself now. There was no way in hell Sebastian would give him the intel they needed now. Not unless Ivy was dead at his feet.

Carson maneuvered through the maze of vehicles, keeping low and moving fast. He searched each one, but Ivy had taken this game of hide-and-seek seriously. A low whine called to him from the right, four rows from the warehouse, and he picked up the pace.

Max's tail set a new speed record as he approached. She danced in excitement of seeing him and to show off her expert skills of protecting the woman at her back.

"How's the leg?" Ivy pressed one side of her body into the rusted-out sedan she'd taken cover behind. Mud caked up her shins and covered her boots, most likely leaving a trail straight to her. It was going to take them working together to get out of this mess.

"I'll live. Thanks for not going for the full monty." Carson struggled to catch his breath as he surveyed the junkyard. Cars stood as silent soldiers all in line, ready to serve. No movement between them, but the moon had disappeared behind a cloud overhead, and his vision had yet to adjust.

"Can't have you slowing me down, can I?" She leaned back to get a view over the rear end of the vehicle. "Where's your friend?"

"South side of the lot. I can give you a head start, but I'm going to have to sell my part." Carson turned on his heels, staying low enough to avoid drawing attention. "I'm sorry about this, Ivy. I failed to account for the cartel recognizing your face."

"It's not your fault I've got such a pretty face. This is God-given." Her attempt to lighten the tension closing in worked, but it didn't last long. The cars in this lot weren't stacked on top of each other. Any move on their part would give away their location. "Still think Sebastian will give us the information we came for?"

"As long as we put you in the position of power." He scratched at Max's head to get her to settle down. "Until we have every last soldier and contact in *Sangre por Sangre* in custody or buried, I'm not sure it's smart to risk my cover. Including Dr. Piel's killer."

"What if we just ask for his identity nicely?" she asked.

"Sure. Let me know how that goes." He caught movement out of the corner of his eye. A mere two rows to their left. Damn it. Carson reached for his weapon, but he'd left their sidearms where he'd tossed them. "Think you can get to your gun if I distract him?"

"This mud isn't very forgiving." She hiked onto her heels, bracing both hands against the sedan. The car wobbled and groaned under the leverage, and he realized all four wheels had been scavenged. The metal body had been suspended by blocks. "But I can make it."

They had to try. Carson wrapped one hand around her arm and pulled her in. Not unlike when he'd crushed her against his chest a few minutes ago. Only this time, his mouth came down on hers. This kiss was quick and desperate, but it was enough to reenergize his nervous system and keep his head in the game. "Take Max. I'll draw him away. Be careful."

Ivy rolled her lips between her teeth in the dim light given off by the moon above. "You, too."

He crouched low and headed farther back in the lot, the opposite direction of Ivy and Max. This would work. It had to work. Because losing her once had nearly killed him and had taken one of his kidneys. He wouldn't recover if something happened to her again. His breathing shallowed as he tried to listen for squelching footsteps, but there was nothing. No sign of Sebastian. No gunshots. No insect noises coming from the desert spanning out on every side of the junkyard.

Everything had gone dead silent.

A barrel of a gun pressed into the back of his head.

Carson froze.

"I knew there had to be someone on the inside. It was the only explanation for how Socorro and the feds managed to find us time and time again." Sebastian's voice no longer held that mentor quality Carson had associated with him. Instead, this was the cartel soldier who would do whatever it took to survive. "On your feet, Rojas."

Without a weapon of his own, Carson didn't have a choice. He failed to catch sight of Ivy or Max as he shoved upward. There was a part of him he'd had to hide from her these past two days. A monster he'd fed with every innocent life taken and order fulfilled within the cartel. It clawed to the surface now, changing him, pushing out all emotion and feeling. "Call me dirty one more time, and I'll feed you that gun, *amigo.*"

He didn't give Sebastian a chance to counter. Dodging to one side, Carson grabbed for the gun, ripped it from the man's hand and took aim. All in the span of a blink of an eye. "This right here? This is what those Socorro dogs want. For us to turn on each other, but we're smarter than that."

He relaxed both hands around the weapon.

"These people have driven us out of our homes and into the ground. They've destroyed our futures, our *familia* and murdered our friends." Carson offered the weapon back. "Don't play into their mind games. Don't give them what they want."

A smile creased Sebastian's mouth, one of pride, as he accepted his weapon. "You always were my favorite, Dominic. Out of all my soldiers, I knew you had a bright future in *Sangre por Sangre.* Come." His mentor navigated down the row of cars, toward the gate blocking Carson's SUV. "The *gringa* isn't going anywhere."

He scoured the visible layout of the junkyard for any

sign of Ivy, but all had gone still. A sick knot twisted in his gut. "What do you mean she isn't going anywhere?"

Sebastian waved the gun over his shoulder. "You think this is how I wanted to spend my retirement? In a junkyard? No, no, no. This place isn't one of the fancy safe houses the lieutenants run to." The cartel soldier lowered his voice, slowed his pace. As though they were approaching a cornered animal. "These cars are part of a maze. They funnel trespassers right where I want them. Like a spider catching a fly in her web."

A bark echoed through the property. Then another. Though Carson didn't have eyes on Max's location or Ivy, he forced himself to remain.

Sebastian brought him to the edge of a dark expanse of dirt tucked between two rows of vehicles. No. Not dirt. A massive hole nearly invisible at this time of night.

And there at the bottom lay his partner. Unconscious. Unmoving. Max circled around Ivy's body, staring up at him for help.

"This is where *el jefe* sent his enemies to be questioned and die." Sebastian smiled, proud of his accomplishment, before turning back to Ivy at the bottom of the hole. "He sent them to me."

Carson didn't have a chance to process what Sebastian meant as his recruiter shoved him forward. The ground rushed to meet him. Too fast. And the world went black.

Chapter Seven

Something grimy coated the inside of her mouth.

Her pulse pounded at the back of her head as she tried to bring herself back into consciousness, but the delirium of sleep worked to drag her back down. There was no pain there. No pounding in her ankle. No headache.

Warmth framed her jaw, turning her face this way and that. Too easily. As though she were nothing but a rag doll. "Come now, *senorita*. It's no fun if you're not awake for this next part."

Next part? What was the next part?

Ivy put everything she had into forcing her eyes open. But the world seemed to have turned upside down while she'd been asleep. Not asleep. Knocked out. The outline of a man shifted in front of her, letting her brain first take in the position of her body. Gravity pulled on her every muscle, pain igniting in her feet. Like they'd fallen asleep. No. Like the blood supply had been cut off.

She dragged her chin to her chest, a feat in and of itself. Upside down. A prickling took hold in her fingers. Her hands had been tied behind her back. With a zip tie, from what she could feel.

"Ah, there we are." The man in front of her took his seat. Though she couldn't pick out any distinguishing features with the lighting so low. Little of her surroundings were distinguishable, but he seemed to be avoiding showing his face altogether. "That's better, don't you think?"

His voice grated against her nerves. The kind of voice that visited in nightmares. Gravelly but calm at the same time. Low and threatening.

Ivy pulled at the zip ties binding her wrists at her lower back. She'd trained her operatives to beat such flimsy safeguards. It wouldn't take much to break through the thin plastic, but the angle had to be right. Upside down was not a good angle. "Where...?"

Snippets of memory—of running for the gate of the junkyard—pieced together as slowly as the puzzle she'd been working on since Christmas. She and Max had gotten sights on the gate. They'd run while Carson intercepted Sebastian. Then...inky blackness.

A hole. Her stomach lurched as she recalled the sensation of falling. She'd landed feetfirst, but her right foot had made contact with a rock protruding from the basin. Her ankle had shot one way while her foot had gone the other before her head had collided with another rock jutting out from the side of the dirt wall. And Max... Where was Max? Where was Carson? "Where am I?"

"Does it matter?" Her captor shifted in his chair, but there was a hint of resistance in the movement. As though his body were fighting against him. She hadn't been able to estimate his age without looking at his face directly, but the thin, papery skin along the backs of his hands said older rather than younger. Crusted jeans were stained with what looked like oil and grease, but from what little light illuminated the room, she noted perfectly clean, trimmed nails.

Not the mechanic he wanted her to believe he was.

Interlacing his hands against his low belly, Sebastian waited. It was an interrogation technique. Silence created pressure to fill the void. Lawyers, law enforcement and her own operatives used it as a weapon, but Ivy was conscious enough to recognize it for what it was: establishing power. He wanted her to believe he was in control. That the only way out of this was to comply, but she'd been through worse. Had survived worse. And he sure as hell would have to try a lot harder to get anything out of her.

Sebastian reached for something off to one side, pulling a sidearm into view. Her sidearm. "No wallet or keys in your possession. Just a gun, a little pocket-knife and a lie about who you are. You failed to realize I knew exactly who you were before you showed up at my gate."

"Then why let me in? Why go through this whole charade?" Ivy tried to take in the rest of the room. Find any potential objects that could be used as a weapon. But despite what her brain wanted this place to be, she couldn't pick out equipment, tools or machinery relating to a junkyard warehouse. No. This place, this room, was something far more dangerous. Unique.

"To cut the head off the snake." Sebastian detached the gun's magazine from the main frame, seemingly counting the bullets lined up like little soldiers inside. "You and your private military contractors have torn *Sangre por Sangre* limb from limb. You've hunted us, stolen from us, murdered us."

"Yes. Well, I'm so sorry about stopping your lieutenants from slaughtering thousands of innocent lives so you can push your drugs, steal their women and children and make a profit off other people's misery." Pure vitriol spread through her at the thought of all the damage the cartel had inflicted. All the hatred they'd created. The families they'd torn apart and the homes they'd destroyed. Raids, explosions, underage recruitment. Socorro had saved lives, and now he was going to try to convince her she was the bad guy? "I won't do it again. Promise."

Sebastian's low laugh brushed against a buried part of her memory. As though she'd heard it before. Except that was impossible. Running Socorro kept her out of the field, and there hadn't been a single instance in which *Sangre por Sangre* had succeeded in getting past her security measures. "I can see why Dominic likes you so much. Why he couldn't kill you himself."

Carson. Her heart jumped into her throat. Nothing in her peripheral vision suggested Carson or Max had been invited to this little party. The lack of windows in this place kept her from deducing how long she'd been unconscious, but her internal hunger cues gave a few clues. Not enough time for her insides to start eating themselves. Couple of hours. Maybe less. Which meant they had to be somewhere else. Somewhere within the warehouse or on the property. Sebastian wouldn't have had time to dispose of their bodies and conduct this worthless interview.

The cartel soldier shifted forward, dark hair coming into view as he stood. Heavy footfalls seemed to echo through her with each connection to the cement floor. Sebastian circled to one side, just out of reach. "I imagine you're the reason for my protégé's recent lack of commitment to the operation. Why he's been so…distracted."

"What can I say? I'm in very high demand." Ivy took the opportunity of being out of his direct sight to study the apparatus keeping her hoisted above the floor. While Sebastian had secured her hands with zip ties, he'd doubled up on chains around her ankles, hanging her from an oversize metal hook used to tow vehicles. And considering Carson most likely hadn't helped secure her for the impending torture coming her way, Sebastian would have needed to lift her in place himself. Meaning he wasn't as invalid as he wanted her to believe.

A fist rocketed into the side of her face.

Lightning exploded behind her eyes. Her teeth cut into the soft tissues of her mouth and forced blood to the surface. Momentum swung her body away from her attacker. Sebastian caught her before the pendulum could be completed, and a visceral stain of evil leached through her clothing and deep into bone from his touch alone. "Why don't you tell me what you managed to get out of Dominic, eh? What was your end goal?"

"If I told you that, I'd have to cut this conversation short." Ivy struggled to breathe through the blood clogging her airway. "And we just started to get to know each other."

Another strike spun her a full one hundred and eighty degrees. Only this time, one of her back teeth dislodged. Her face pulsed in anger. The adrenaline that had numbed the area was already dissipating, and pain moved in to replace it. Her vision wavered. She fisted her hands in an attempt to stay conscious, but there were no guarantees.

Searing pain spread across her scalp as Sebastian pulled her head back by her hair. Exposing her throat. A small blade pricked at the thin skin there as he got close enough to whisper in her ear. "You know, I've seen a pocketknife like this before. A few years ago now. You don't realize how very sharp they are until someone stabs you with it."

Warning pooled in her gut.

"I know why you came here, Agent Bardot." Puffs of air tickled her ear and triggered a shiver, but she wouldn't let him see the effect he had on her. That his proximity had on her. "I know you've been searching for me all this time. That I'm the one who haunts your dreams and influenced every decision you've ever made in the past two years. You built Socorro to protect yourself from me, but where is your team now? Hmm?"

Agent Bardot. Not *Ms*.

Ice coursed through her veins as that voice took its rightful place in her memory. There was a reason it had felt so familiar, why he'd tried to hide his identity.

Sebastian moved into her line of view, fully exposing his face in the light, and her insides knotted tight.

"You." All this time, Carson had been tasked to uncover the identity of the man who'd killed three women from within *Sangre por Sangre*. And the son of a bitch had been in front of him the entire time. Though it wasn't clear until this moment—hanging upside down from her ankles with blood trailing into her hairline—that Carson hadn't set eyes on the man who'd nearly killed her.

That night, those memories she'd tried to bury, flooded through her mind in a rush that stole her breath. Of waking in a basement not unlike this room, of feeling the killer's hands on her. Of knowing there was a possibility she would die, that she'd never see her partner again. In an instant, Ivy was right back in that position. Vulnerable, helpless. It was all too much of a reminder of those nights her stepfather had drunk too much and exerted his power over her mother with flying fists, hard shoves and broken bones.

Until she hadn't been able to take it anymore.

Ivy saw herself in her mind's eye pulling her stepdad's gun from his nightstand as a ten-year-old. She saw herself fisting her pocketknife in that basement two years ago.

And in this moment, she saw herself snapping through the zip tie binding her wrists and ending this for good.

"That's right, *senorita*. Me." Sebastian released his hold on her hair, letting the blade of her own pocketknife cut through the first layer of skin at her neck. "You and I have some unfinished business to attend to."

ALL HE COULD hear was barking.

Incessant and sharp and panicked.

Carson felt as though an elephant was sitting on his

chest, ready to crush him to death. He tried to reorient himself, but he couldn't seem to get his body to obey. The last memory—of falling, of being shoved, of trying to avoid landing on Ivy—took center stage.

Sebastian. That son of a bitch had captured Ivy and Max. And now… Now Carson didn't know what had happened to his partner. Though from the sound of it, Max wasn't too far away. Her barks cleared the haze from his head second by second.

He tried to bring his head up. Too fast. His forehead collided with something metal and large. Lightning exploded behind his eyes, and he fell back. Cement smacked against the back of his skull. If he hadn't sustained a concussion from the fall into a dark hole in the middle of a salvage yard, he sure as hell had now.

His next inhalation caught hints of motor oil, gasoline and rust. His chest seemed to fill any available space, but it was too dark to get a sense of his situation. It was like he'd been sandwiched between two oversize forces. Carson maneuvered his hands at his sides. His weapon had been taken from him. Sebastian hadn't wanted to take any chances of him shooting his way out of…whatever this place was. Not a surprise but still a disappointment. He'd been positioned on his back. Cement beneath him had been sealed. Most likely a floor. Inside the warehouse? He couldn't be sure yet.

Another round of barking pierced into awareness.

"Max?" Carson's vision adjusted the longer he focused, but there was still too much unknown for him to create a strategy to get out. Her responding whine confirmed what he needed to know. She was alive. She was okay. "Good girl."

He managed to get his elbows into his rib cage and feel the wall hoisted above him. He followed the curves of what felt like car parts. Only there was something distorted about their shape. As though they'd been crushed. Burned crust flaked off and fell into his eyes, nose and mouth. He spit at the chemical bite, but there was nothing that could get rid of the taste of asphalt and heat. "Damn it."

Sebastian had pinned him beneath a crushed car somehow.

The narrow cavity giving him enough space to keep breathing must've been maintained by one of the hoists. Though the son of a bitch had set it on the lowest level. Without the vehicle's tires, there was no room to navigate an escape.

He was trapped.

An animal-like scream escaped his chest as Carson shoved against the vehicle balanced above him with everything he had. It echoed off the warehouse walls but failed to change anything. He needed to get out of here. He needed to locate Ivy.

He'd brought her here to ease the pressure of this investigation, to give her hope the past two years hadn't been for nothing. But all he'd managed to do was make things worse. He'd trusted the wrong person, and now she would be the one to pay for his mistake.

Carson braced both palms against the underside of the car. The muscles in his neck and shoulders strained against the weight of the vehicle. There was no moving it. Not on his own. "Come on!"

There was no telling what Sebastian would do to Ivy. How much pain he would inflict. Or if the bastard would just kill her for her connection to Socorro.

Max's barking seared his nerves with every protest. Until it was all he could focus on. His heart rate ratcheted into his throat as he released his hold on the vehicle above. He couldn't lose Ivy. Not after everything they'd fought for. Not after what they'd survived. They'd sacrificed too much to only come this far and get nothing in reward. He didn't want to imagine all the ways Sebastian was punishing her for her crimes against the cartel, but he couldn't stop the thoughts either.

He'd taken this assignment to do something good with his life. To earn the kidneys both his mother and Ivy had donated to save his life. But what had he really accomplished? What did he have to show for it? There was no end to the amount of evil and violence he and Ivy took on every day, and no matter how hard he fought, it felt as though every step forward was ripped out from underneath him. He'd given up his friends, what little remained of his family, his life. All he had left was Ivy.

"And Max." Carson shifted his body weight to one side of the cavity stabilizing the hoist. There wasn't enough room for him to roll. He had to leverage his heels and palms into the floor and slide. Dim light bled through the gaps between the crushed vehicle and the platform meant to support the tires. He could make out movement through the holes. "Max."

Stillness followed her gruff response.

More details came into focus the longer he forced his brain to account for the obstacles in his vision. He could just make out the K-9's paws if he concentrated hard enough. "Come here."

Max took a few steps forward but was prevented from making it to his position. Which meant Sebastian had most likely tied her to something in the shop. Only Carson couldn't tell with what. There was a difference between a chain and a section of rope. She whined about not being able to fulfill her orders. "It's okay. We're going to get out of here. We're going to find your mom. I promise."

Though how he was going to do any of that still hadn't made itself clear. Either way, he wouldn't give up. Not on them. Not on their future. One they'd earned through the countless hours of blood, sweat and tears. Of losses on both sides and the hurt they'd inflicted. On victims who hadn't been given the justice they deserved. Because he believed in them. Him and Ivy. These past two years had been about doing what they each thought was best to protect those who couldn't protect themselves, but no future was worth not having her in it.

Carson angled his head in a way to give him a better view of whatever had been tied around Max's collar. An earthquake-sized relief rocked through him. Rope. He and Max had trained for this in the times they weren't assigned perimeter security or guard duty. It had taken up silent hours waiting until the next Socorro raid, and he'd never been more grateful for those hours now. "Max, *packen*." Bite.

The German shepherd stared at him as though trying to decipher if a crushed car was the one giving her the order. Carson fit his finger through one of the gaps in the metal. *"Packen."*

His K-9 partner took the command to heart, turning on the section of rope securing her to something out of sight. She clamped down on the twine and got to work. Within minutes, Max had chewed through the rope and gained her freedom. A few feet of rope still remained tied to her collar, but she didn't seem to mind. Charging for his position, she put some bounce in her step. Showing off. She pressed her nose against his exposed finger.

"Good girl. Good girl. I'm getting you the largest steak I can find as soon as we get out of this place." Carson rubbed at her nose, but the affection fell short. "Okay. We need to find the controls to get this thing off of me."

How the hell he was going to manage that in his current position, he didn't know, but Max was smart, and he'd prepared her for anything. He didn't have a whole lot of knowledge when it came to mechanic shops and salvage yards, but there had to be a button or lever that would lift the vehicle. *"Knopf."* Button.

Max sniffed at his finger for a few more seconds, then pulled back. Out of sight. Her nails clicked against the cracking cement. Strong at first, then less so. A rise of panic coated Carson's throat, but as long as he was trapped here, Max wouldn't leave. It wasn't in her nature to abandon the people she loved.

"What do you see, Max?" He tried to maneuver farther down the cavity, but the angle of the tire platform dropped off toward his feet, and his toes hit the underside of the vehicle. *"Knopf?"*

No answer. No sound of her nails on the floor.

"Max?" he asked.

The car jolted above him.

His nerves spiked into dangerous territory. Carson braced for the potential of the two-ton vehicle to drop directly on him, but nothing happened for a series of seconds.

The car shifted again. This time increasing the light coming in through the gaps between the hunk of metal and the hoist. It was moving upward. A laugh clawed through Carson's chest. "Max, *knopf*!"

A mechanical groan filled his ears, and the car lifted higher. It cleared the platform, but there still wasn't enough room for him to squeeze through. Not yet. "Keep going, baby." Another round of moaning raised the oversize paperweight higher.

The hoist continued its upward ascent. Any mechanic would've spotted the signs the weight had been unevenly distributed and stopped, but he couldn't expect that from a German shepherd.

The vehicle had started tipping toward him. Off-balance.

But there still wasn't enough space between the bottom of the car and the tire platform for him to escape. Carson didn't have a choice. He had to move. Now.

He kept his attention locked on the unbalanced vehicle as he hauled himself over the brim of the cavity holding him hostage.

Carson hit the cement floor, free of his makeshift prison.

Just as the vehicle dropped.

Two thousand–plus pounds of metal screeched from the impact. In the exact same location as he'd been held hostage. Shattered glass escaped the confines of the car's shell and skimmed across the floor to his position.

Max's bark called to him from the back of the hoist. He scrambled to his feet, out of breath and in one piece. Because of his K-9 partner. Max nearly knocked him over as she stretched onto her hind legs to give her version of a hug. He buried his hands into her fur. "You're getting as many steaks as you want tonight."

She licked at his face, then sneezed from the amount of crust that covered his skin, before dropping onto all fours.

"Had I known you were going to kiss me, I would've showered first." He caught sight of a toolbox splayed open with an array of potential weapons. Sebastian might've taken his gun, but the son of a bitch wasn't going to take anything else from him. Carson collected a heavy wrench capable of a lot of damage if swung hard enough. "Now, what do you say we go get your mom?"

Chapter Eight

The crash jolted her awake.

Though she wasn't entirely sure she'd fallen asleep as Sebastian—if that was his real name—fed into his own desperation for answers. Where was her team? Where would they strike next? Had they learned about this location? Her body hurt. Every inch. Blood dripped from her hair onto the floor below, staining the cement.

A bark reached through the haze closing in around Ivy's awareness. Through the seal her brain had created to protect itself. She knew that bark.

"I never liked that dog." Sebastian stepped into view, her pocketknife in hand. Coated with her blood.

"She's a...good judge of character." She'd lost count of how many lacerations he'd cut into her arms, legs and stomach. Nothing vital. He knew what he was doing, how to bleed her to death without so much as raising her body's alarm systems until it was too late. Her mouth felt full. As though she'd attempted to swallow a handful of bees. Adrenaline had left the party a while ago. She couldn't count on it to get her out of this as she had so many times before. Adrenaline didn't consider logic or others. It was pure survival. Her arms ached as she attempted to break through the zip ties one more time. In vain. The angle was wrong. Not enough force.

"Don't go anywhere. We're not finished." He flipped the pocketknife to face down in his palm and stabbed it into the drywall near a door she hadn't noticed until then. In a single breath, her abductor—her torturer— was gone.

A sliver of hope that had no business sparking lit up inside of her. The crash. She wasn't sure of the source, but given Max was alive, Ivy was willing to bet Carson was, too. That he'd been the one to cause the disruption of Sebastian's latest masterpiece. Ivy struggled against gravity and exhaustion to duck her chin into her chest. There wasn't much she could do in the way of getting her hands around her feet for better access.

But there was another way.

She forced air into her lungs, then breathed out harder than necessary. It had been years since she'd dislocated her shoulder, courtesy of her stepfather, but old wounds never really healed right. There was a chance this could work. If she was willing to endure just a little longer. For Carson. For Max. For the family she'd created in a world full of nothing but brutality and betrayal. Ivy clamped her back teeth together, stretching her bound wrists toward the floor.

The idea of inflicting pain on herself when she'd intentionally built Socorro to protect her and others from going through what she had as a child gripped her hard. But the possibility of losing everything—her partner, her team, her dog—hurt so much more.

"One." Her stomach protested the pain coming. "Two."

She bounced her straightened arms to get a feel for the momentum needed. "Three."

She put everything she had into disconnecting her right shoulder. The muscles screamed as they twisted in the entirely wrong direction. Inky blackness encroached into the edges of her vision, but she had to hang on. She had to keep going. Her wrists followed the path of the zip tie as she brought them forward. Every breath helped ease the pain, but her body had hit a wall. It couldn't take much more.

Ivy fought through the drowning sensation pulling her into unconsciousness. If she blacked out now, Sebastian would have free rein to kill her and everyone she loved. There would be no one to stop him. No. She couldn't give in. No matter how much she wanted to. She'd survived before. She could—she would—do it again.

Reaching for her feet, she attempted to curl her upper body forward. But the lacerations across her midsection only slowed her down. She fell back and let the relief take hold. Just for a moment. There was a chance she'd never be able to lift a weapon with her damaged arm, but for now, all she needed it to do was get her closer to the tow hook holding her hostage. Ivy tried again. A groan backed up in her throat as her fingertips brushed the end of the hook.

"Closer." She collapsed again. The room swirled in her vision as she released the air she hadn't realized she'd been holding on to. Time seemed to slip through her fingers without any effort. Seconds, minutes, an hour. She wasn't sure how long she hung there. The rhythmic patter of blood dripping onto the floor kept in time with the pulse thudding in her throat. This wasn't how it was supposed to end.

She pried her eyes open.

And stared straight into the face of a dead man. As real as Sebastian, as Carson, as the operatives on her team. He hadn't aged a day despite twenty-seven years since she'd seen him.

"What did I always tell you, Ives?" her stepfather said. "You're not strong enough to beat me."

"You're not real." The words slurred due to the swelling in her face and lips. "You're not here."

His sneer pooled dread at the base of her spine. It was that same sneer he'd given her when he'd dared her to pull the trigger that night. Right before he'd lunged at her to take the gun. She'd shot him at just ten years old, scared, desperate to help her mother, to keep him from killing them both. Then she'd shot him again. He'd dropped to the floor right there in the entryway of their small Jacksonville house, hand to his chest. And she'd stood over him, watching. Waiting for him to take his last breath. Her mother had called the paramedics with a broken arm and two missing teeth, and the EMTs had somehow kept him alive. Only he'd never come home after leaving the hospital. He was still out there. Still haunting her memories, her nightmares.

"You're a coward, Ives. Same as you've always been." Her stepfather moved in closer. So close, she could almost smell that sickening scent of his aftershave. "You think you're protecting people, but the truth is, you're just protecting yourself. Like a child. All you ever cared about was yourself, what you wanted. That's why you shot me. It wasn't to protect your mama. Look what happened to her after that night."

"No." Tears burned in her eyes, giving away the echoing feelings of helplessness when faced with this particular threat. She didn't want to think about that. About how after the incident her mother hadn't been able to find a job, how she hadn't been able to put food on the table and then just gave up trying. Life had beaten her mother down long after her stepfather had gone, had stolen any glimpse of hope. Until there was nothing left but drugs, a revolving door of men and a final overdose.

"She died because of you. You know that, right?" His words surfaced and took shape from within; they'd followed her through high school, college, into the FBI, and were controlling her now. "If you hadn't shot me, she'd still be here. You're pathetic, Ivy Bardot. You're nothing. You can't save anyone. You can't even save yourself."

"Stop." Tears mixed with blood across her face. The image—the hallucination—of her stepfather waned. Years of building her personal armor, of becoming the woman she was, seemed to disintegrate at the accusations living in her head. Ivy shook her head as though it would make him go away. "It's not true."

The thing that made everything not so bad was knowing, sooner or later, I was coming home to you. Carson's words cut through the self-hatred and worked to repair the damage done to her heart. They burned through her, cleansing and clarifying. Ivy set her attention on the figment of her imagination. Carson was out there right now. Fighting to survive. Fighting for her. Just as he'd done during their last case together. They were still here because they'd refused to give up on one another. And she wasn't going to let the past stand in the way now.

"You're wrong." Confidence replenished some of the strength she'd lost since coming to this hellhole. "I was a child, asshole. Everything that happened in our family was the responsibility of two adults who should've made better choices."

Anger creased her stepfather's expression. He reached for her, but Ivy thrust herself upward with everything she had left. Her fingers latched on to the tow hook. She gripped the cold steel with force enough to crush a diamond, hauling her bound ankles over the lip of the hook. Just as quickly, her strength gave out. She hit the floor, her legs collapsing out from under her. It was enough. She was free.

Her stepfather had returned to the small space in her head where she'd buried the memories of him. At least he'd been good for something after all this time. She managed to untangle her ankles from the rope, but the filaments of torn muscle in her shoulder wouldn't like what came next. Hiking her hands above her head, she slammed them down against her thighs with as much force as she could muster. The zip tie broke. Setting sights on the door, she fought through the dizziness closing in and locked on her pocketknife stabbed into the drywall there. "That's mine."

Crusted blood stained the handle and blade, but it would be enough in the coming fight. Because this wasn't over. Throwing open the door, Ivy stepped out into a black expanse of warehouse. Her ankle ached under her full weight, but she couldn't stop now. She had a family to protect. Every cell in her body homed in on picking up the threat before it slapped her in the face. A single fluorescent light flickered at her left, and she scanned for movement.

"You were right, Sebastian." Her words bounced off the sheet-metal walls, and the confidence in her voice invigorated her to keep moving. "You and I have unfinished business."

No answer. No sign of Max or Carson. It would be easy to panic if she let herself, but she'd just conquered one of the demons that kept her up at night. Now it was time to face the second. Gripping her pocketknife in her nondominant hand, she pressed her back into the walls of whatever room Sebastian had held her in. "Come out, come out, wherever you are."

"Are you sure you want to play this game, little girl?" Sebastian's answer felt far away and yet too close at the same time. "The last time I checked, you weren't cut out to face me."

She'd sustained a good amount of injury hung upside down as his personal punching bag. Her brain could be messing with her, but Ivy got the feeling her perception hadn't changed. Sebastian knew this warehouse better than she or Carson. There were spaces he'd most likely created to track his enemies, watch them, ambush them. He wouldn't be so lucky today. Memories of that voice threatened to slow her down, but she'd already made up her mind. There was no turning back.

A shadow shifted in her peripheral vision.

She didn't hesitate. She arced the blade of her under-sized weapon.

And hit something soft.

"My pocketknife says otherwise." Ivy fisted Sebastian's collar and dragged him into the light. Victory charged through her as pain creased into his face. "This is for Nafessa Piel."

Agony seared through her side. Exposing a thin saw blade where her right kidney used to be.

"And this is for stabbing me two years ago," he said.

She stumbled back, forced to leave her pocketknife in his shoulder.

And dropped to her knees.

"No!" CARSON WATCHED on as though things unraveled in slow motion.

Ivy pressed a hand to her side. Then turned her gaze to him down the length of the maze of in-progress auto-mobiles before going limp. She hit the floor with noth-ing more than the sound of a feather landing lightly.

Everything in him froze. His worst nightmare had come to fruition. He'd lost her. Carson's bellow filled the entire warehouse.

Sebastian wasn't ready for the rage boiling over in-side of him.

Carson raced to close the distance between them. He swung the heavy-duty wrench with every ounce of con-trol he had left. Sebastian dodged the first attempt but couldn't avoid the second. Metal connected with bone in a sickening crunch that would haunt Carson for the rest of his life. The man he'd once considered a mentor within the cartel—a friend, even—had taken away the only person he had left. There was no one left to ground him to this life. His father had left when he'd been a kid; his mother had died after an infection started eating her from the inside. The FBI wanted nothing to do with him, and the men and women he'd fought beside on the battlefield were six feet underground. And now Ivy. Taken by the very person he'd saved from being buried under megatons of rock, cement and steel.

He swung the wrench back for another blow. To end it.

Only Sebastian wasn't ready to accept his fate. The cartel soldier caught Carson's wrist, but the wrench's momentum ripped the tool out of Carson's hand. It skidded across the cement and was lost to shadow in an instant.

A fist rocketed into Carson's face. Once. Twice. Lights exploded behind his eyes, but it wouldn't slow him down. Sebastian held on to his wrist. Except there was more than one way to win a fight. Carson thrust his forehead into the bastard's face. *Sangre por Sangre*'s most fearsome killer fell back, releasing his hold with a groan. Another fist came at him, and Carson raised both forearms to block it.

"Max, *bring*!" Retrieve. The K-9 leaped from her hiding place with a sharp protest, vaulting for Ivy. She'd never had to pull an entire person out of a hostile situation before, but Carson had his faith placed in her. It was the only way they were all going to get out of this alive. The German shepherd latched on to Ivy's boot and started jerking Ivy out of sight.

"I'm going to cut you and gut you for what you've done, Rojas. You should know better by now. No one escapes *Sangre por Sangre*." Sebastian added some distance between them, swiping the back of his hand beneath his shattered nose.

"What did you just say?" That phrasing. He'd heard it before. No. He'd read it before. Carved into the backs of four women, one of whom had been killed a mere two days ago. But…it wasn't possible. Was it? The man standing in front of him—who'd served as his recruiter and guided him through the ranks of the cartel—couldn't be the same one he'd been searching for all this time.

"There's no saving Agent Bardot. Even if you make it out of here alive, I will hunt you both for the rest of your lives." Sebastian's threats were more growl than words now. "You will never be safe. You will never have a future. I'll make sure of it."

Agent Bardot. Not Ivy Bardot of Socorro Security. Sebastian had known Ivy since before she'd founded her private military contractor operation. But it didn't matter what the son of a bitch called her. Every second Carson wasted here was another second Ivy didn't have. She'd been stabbed. He didn't know how badly, but he'd lived through the experience enough to tell him there was a chance she could bleed out if he didn't get to her.

"We've survived worse than you." Carson kicked out. His heel connected with Sebastian's midsection and sent the cartel soldier straight back into a tool bench.

"You have no idea who I am, do you, boy? What I can do to you and your partner?" Sebastian grabbed for a section of chain coiled on the surface and whipped the heavy metal. He was grabbing for anything and everything. Always putting his own survival first. It was a wonder Carson had gotten this far within *Sangre por Sangre* without seeing it until now. "You've never known the kind of pain I will bring down on you."

Sebastian lashed out with the chain.

The links snapped against Carson's raised wrist as he attempted to block the strike and coiled around as tight as a boa constrictor might. Muscles burned as he, in turn, pulled the chain tighter and brought Sebastian into his personal space.

A fist thrust into his kidney.

Carson arched backward as the pain lightninged across his back and down into his legs. Three surgeries—two transplants and a stab wound—should have prepared him for the pain, but the opposite seemed to be true. One knee bit into the ground. Sebastian released his hold on the chain. Only to secure it around Carson's neck in his next breath.

The metal dug into Carson's flesh. Pinched his skin between the links as his air supply lodged in his throat. He couldn't breathe. Couldn't think. Pressure built in his chest to the point he was convinced his lungs might pop. He tried to twist out of the man's grip, but Sebastian only held on tighter.

Black waves pierced into his vision. Trying to convince him to give up, to sink into the gravitational pull of unconsciousness. Carson threaded his fingers around the chain, but it was no use. Sebastian had the upper hand. He put everything he had into his heels, kicking back. But the leverage did nothing to relieve the weight of suffocation.

Sebastian's hands shook from the effort. The only reminder the cartel recruiter was human. That he could bleed just as well as Carson. As Ivy.

Max would get her out of the warehouse. She and Ivy were going to make it. His partner had out-strategized some of the top supervising agents back in the FBI. When she set the rules, failure wasn't an option. There was only winning in her book. And she wouldn't let something like a stab wound slow her down. Not when there were potential lives at risk. The partners who'd come before him had seen her as a narcissist, selfish, someone bent on having control and only concerned with her own survival. He'd been warned of her intensity, that she tended to mow people down—partners, witnesses, supervising agents—to get her way.

But that wasn't Ivy at all. Not the real her. Not the woman she'd allowed him to see underneath that battle armor. Though it had taken both of them nearly dying for Carson to see the truth. That intensity every one of her former partners had feared had been built on survival. They'd been right about that. But not hers. She fought for the victims. For the potential victims. For those who'd been taken advantage of and those too scared to stand up for themselves. She fought a war no one else could see to ensure the evil would never touch them. Hell, he admired her. Wanted to be half as strong as her.

And he would make sure she got out of this alive.

Because the cartel wouldn't stop, and the innocent

lives in their path deserved someone to protect them. They needed her to keep fighting for them. She was all that mattered.

Carson grabbed for the old man's forearms with both hands. Sebastian had the upper hand, the higher ground, but Carson had the strength. He put everything he had into shoving to his feet. Sebastian was forced to adjust his hold.

And Carson took advantage.

He hauled the cartel soldier over his back and slammed the bastard onto the cement in front of him. Air crushed from Sebastian's lungs as Carson unraveled the chain from around his neck. His cough filled the warehouse as his lungs tried to remember how to breathe. He tossed the length of chain. "You're not strong enough to take her on alone. No one is. So tell upper management if they want a war, they'll have it, and they will lose. Because you have no idea what you're up against."

The old man grabbed for his back, rolling onto one side. Giving up the fight.

Carson stepped over the son of a bitch, and exhaustion hit hard. He'd been running off fumes and adrenaline. A potent combination that only inflicted more damage the longer he pushed himself. He located the point where Ivy had collapsed, noting the trail of blood left behind as Max had dragged her out of the building. He had to go. He had to get her to the hospital. Now.

"You don't get to walk away from this. None of us do." Sebastian's voice was the only warning Carson received as a pipe came down on his shoulder.

The pain exploded through his neck and down his

arm, but it wasn't enough to stop him from turning on his former mentor. He caught the pipe on Sebastian's second attempt and ripped the weapon from the man's hand. Immediately returning the attack. The end of the pipe connected with Sebastian's face, and the son of a bitch hit the floor. "Go back into hiding, Sebastian. That's the only way you're going to get out of this alive."

He tossed the pipe to one side, jogging for the exit. The trail of blood took a right turn. Headed straight for the nearest door. "Good girl, Max."

Carson shoved through the barrier and out in the New Mexico sunrise. Cold air burned down his throat as he sighted the German shepherd struggling to get her human across the salvage yard gravel. His heart double-timed as he picked up the pace. "Ivy."

Max released her hold on Ivy, pouncing on all four paws.

He skidded to a stop, kicking up gravel as he hauled Ivy's upper body away from the ground. Her head fell back. Swelling blocked out one of her eyes, bruises already starting across her jaw. But it was the blood that nearly stopped his heart.

Cuts covered her arms, legs and torso. Dozens of them. Something dangerous and more familiar than he wanted to admit clawed through him, and if Ivy weren't in a position of bleeding out in his arms, he would go back into that warehouse. He would make Sebastian pay for what he'd done.

But he didn't have time. Ivy didn't have time. Carson threaded his arms behind her shoulders and knees and shoved to stand. Max followed on his heels, her attention fixed on the woman in his grasp. "I've got you, partner. I've got you."

Chapter Nine

People were dying to get into their graves.

Ivy wasn't one of them.

Bright fluorescent lighting agitated the migraine somehow behind her eyes and every other inch of her brain. She wanted to go back to sleep, but the damn rhythmic pulse on the EKG machine wouldn't let her. The IV line in the back of her hand itched and hurt at the same time. And the bedsheets had obviously come straight from hell.

Ugh. She'd been admitted to a hospital.

"You're awake. That's a good sign." The voice she expected was not the one speaking to her now. Styled dark hair consumed her attention. Not a single hair out of place. White coat—physician.

"I don't know you." Her heart hurt at the reminder Dr. Piel wouldn't be the one to clear her for fieldwork or to go head-to-head with Congress again. Ivy scanned the room, but there was no sign of her team. No sign of Max. Or Carson.

She didn't know what to think of that right then. Didn't really want to think about it.

"No. I expect you wouldn't." Her doctor faced her,

his clipboard leveraged against his lower abdomen. Sharp features built out a handsome face. A little too perfect for her taste. She'd always been attracted to men who had a little wear on them, a little life experience. This one was brand-new. "I'm Dr. Cavill. I'm your attending physician during your stay here."

"And where exactly is here?" Ivy tried to sit up, but her body seemed to have other plans. In the way it screamed at the slightest movement. How her right shoulder refused to take any weight. She could see out of both eyes. That was comforting. The swelling she'd sustained from Sebastian's fist colliding with her face multiple times had gone down. Which meant she hadn't just taken a nap in the time she'd passed out and woken here. It was now most likely days since she and Carson had stepped into a fight they hadn't been prepared to handle.

"Alpine Valley." Dr. Cavill made a note on the clipboard. Presumably in her chart.

"I'm in the clinic." That explained the sheets. Alpine Valley, while home to almost two thousand residents, kept a small-time feel with family-owned businesses and a medical clinic that mostly handled broken bones and people who knew each other's names. "Can I get an early checkout?"

"I'm afraid not." His laugh did nothing to ease her discomfort. "You're lucky to be alive, Ms. Bardot. You've suffered from multiple blows to the face, dislocated a shoulder, and we can't forget about that nasty stab wound in your side. If you still had a kidney, we probably wouldn't be having this conversation."

"Don't forget the sprained ankle." Her nerves were

ticking higher with every pulse of that damn machine. She'd never liked being held against her will. Though she'd have to say this was far more preferable than being hung upside down from a tow hook and used as a piñata. "As for the kidney, someone else is borrowing it."

Dr. Cavill set the clipboard on the side table and unwound the stethoscope from around his neck. Practiced movements. As though done thousands of times. Maybe he wasn't so brand-new after all. "Yes, I've read your medical history."

Goose pimples spread over her skin as he slipped the cold metal between her shoulder blades. She tried to keep her breathing steady, but the more she tried to force herself to relax, the farther away she seemed to get from her goal. "Not sure how you would, seeing as how that is confidential information."

"I contacted your employer when we couldn't find any next of kin to ask permission for your history. One of your employees—Cash, I think his name was—was kind enough to send it over while you were recovering. He's in the lobby with a couple police officers waiting to take your statement about how you ended up in my clinic. Along with what I believe is everyone else who works for Socorro." Dr. Cavill withdrew his probing and recentered the stethoscope around his neck.

Her team was here?

"I have to say it's a miracle the damage you sustained wasn't any worse. The dozen or so lacerations over your body were all relatively surface cuts. We've cleaned and bandaged each one." The physician picked up his clipboard once again, making another note. "As for the stab wound, we sewed you up with two levels of stitches. We found some rust flakes in the wound, so we made sure you were up-to-date on your tetanus shot. You should make a full recovery with no ongoing issues as long as you take it easy for the next few weeks, but based off your past X-rays, I'm willing to bet this isn't the first time you've dislocated that shoulder."

Her past X-rays. Dr. Piel had insisted on collecting as much past medical history and films as possible for each Socorro operative. Ivy couldn't even remember the number of broken bones she'd sustained the first ten years of her life. Each had healed, in their own way. None perfectly. "No. Not the first time."

A deep ache that had nothing to do with her injuries took hold. "What happened to the man who was with me? Carson—" She had to stop herself. Because Carson Lang didn't exist anymore. That part of his life had ended a long time ago, and there was no getting it back. Not as long as *Sangre por Sangre* still had power. "Dominic Rojas. He would've had a German shepherd with him. Is he here?"

"He was." Dr. Cavill finally looked up from that damn clipboard. He pointed to the door with the end of his pen. "I think one of the nurses finally convinced him you would be okay if he got a few hours of sleep. I'll see if my staff can locate him."

Something released inside of her. He was alive. They both were, and it didn't escape Ivy that they'd been in this situation before. Not that long ago they'd faced a killer in a cartel hideout. The same killer. A sinking sensation interrupted the steady rhythm of her heart rate on the EKG, but Dr. Cavill didn't seem to notice.

"Try to get some rest. You've been through a lot." The physician headed for the door. "I'll be back to check on you in a couple hours. Until then, try not to make matters worse by thinking you can check yourself out, Ms. Bardot."

Before he could exit, Dr. Cavill stepped back as the heavy metal door opened from the other side. Carson. "Well, that saves me having to track anyone down."

The doctor closed the door behind him, sealing her and Carson in the same room.

"Hi." As a professional, she ran a multibillion-dollar security firm. She lobbied for additional resources from the Pentagon. She shot down congressmen and made public statements. And the only thing she could think to say when seeing her partner was *hi*.

"You're awake." Carson moved deeper into the room, heading straight for the side of her bed.

"That's what they tell me." She grabbed on to her injured shoulder wrapped securely against her chest. "Can't say it's been a great experience thus far, but it's better than being used as a punching bag for a cartel soldier."

He settled on the edge of the bed, the mattress dipping under his weight, but there was a distance between them. Something thick and unspoken she didn't want to deal with right now. "Ivy, I'm sorry. I made a mistake—"

"Stop. It's…" Well, it wasn't fine. It wasn't close to fine, but blaming him for what had happened wouldn't get them closer to bringing Dr. Piel's killer to justice. "It's him, Carson. Sebastian. He killed those women."

Understanding slid into his expression. "All this time I've been looking for the man who abducted you—almost killed you—and he was standing right in front of me."

"What better way to hide than in plain sight?" Images kept coming back to her. Of the warehouse. Of seeing Carson before she collapsed. There were sensations and memories and confusion. And it had all led to this. To them. Ivy shut down a shiver prickling along her spine. "Did you...? Is he dead?"

"No." Regret laced that single word. "I sent him back to upper management with a message. They want to come for you, they'll lose. I'll make sure of it."

The wrongness of that statement collided with her need to know she wasn't alone in this and pressed the oxygen from her lungs. A warning that had been there since the moment she'd found him in her apartment slithered into awareness. It had taken a back seat in her subconscious over the course of two days, but it was growing now. "You had the chance to put an end to this, and you let the killer off with a warning?"

"You'd been stabbed, Ivy. You were bleeding everywhere. I wasn't sure how long you had until..." Color drained from his face. "I didn't want to lose you again. I did what I thought was right."

Right. Of course he had. Because that was what partners were supposed to do. Ivy chastised herself for seeing a potential threat where there was none. She didn't know whether it was from the painkillers or the trauma she'd sustained that raised her defenses, but there had to be a point where she let herself take something at face value. There wasn't always a hidden agenda. She reached for his hand, pressing her thumb between his first two knuckles. "Thank you. For getting me out of there."

"Actually, that was Max," he said. "Turns out she's a lot better at retrieval than I gave her credit for."

"I'll be sure to thank her, too." Ivy pulled on his hand until Carson's upper body had to come with him.

"You're going to have a hard time getting her attention with all your operatives keeping her busy out in the parking lot." A smile pulled at one corner of his mouth, instantly erasing the memory of Dominic Rojas. The partner she'd fallen for locked his gaze on hers as he leaned into her.

"In that case, I think we should enjoy this time we have alone together," she said.

"Believe me, Agent Bardot." Carson pressed his mouth against hers, and the pain, reality and a whole lot of bad disappeared at the contact. "I intend to."

THEY COULDN'T GO back to the cartel safe house.

Not as long as Sebastian—or whoever the hell the killer was—was alive. Whatever remained of *Sangre por Sangre* had been called to a final fight, with Sebastian at the forefront. There was no going back. There was no more Dominic Rojas or the connection he'd built over the past two years. No resources. No team he could rely on. And Carson couldn't help but feel a hole beginning to develop at an entire two years of his life gone just like that.

Once they'd given their statements to Alpine PD,

they'd been permitted to leave the clinic. As long as Ivy promised to rest. An impossible task for a woman determined to take on the weight of every suffering human and find a dozen solutions in the process. He pulled the SUV off to the side of the road of a little neighborhood he hadn't stepped foot in since he'd gone undercover. Max's tail hit him in the face as she climbed over the center console and across Ivy's lap to look out the window. "Get out of here, you giant fur ball." He tried to maneuver her into the back seat, but there was no derailing the German shepherd.

She was home.

"What are we doing here?" Ivy studied the small house with its pristine stucco, traditional-style roof and maintained front lawn. The tree out front looked much bigger than he remembered the last time he'd been here, and the garage had been painted black instead of its original white, but everything else pulled memories from a happier time.

A time when he knew who the hell he was. Where he belonged.

The bruising along one side of Ivy's face had darkened to a sickening purple and blue but told him Sebastian favored his right hook. Something to keep in mind the next time they met. "You realize I don't live here anymore, right? I live part-time in that place full of bullet holes we escaped four nights ago and the other part in a stronghold with a team of mercenaries."

Carson shouldered out of the vehicle. His forearms ached with the use of the small muscles extending from his wrists to his elbows. Protecting his head from being bashed in with a pipe had left its stain beneath his skin, but it was nothing compared to the pain Ivy had to deal with. They needed somewhere she would be safe, that gave her the time she needed to recover. Where nobody could find her. Rounding in front of the SUV, he felt Ivy's eyes follow him as he approached her door. He opened the passenger-side door and offered his hand. "Trust me."

Max took the opportunity to spring out of the vehicle. She bounded up the driveway and pranced around the front yard as if she owned the place.

Ivy stared at his hand, then cut her gaze to the house behind him. He could practically see the wheels turning in her head, considering all her options. Trust him or die at the hands of a killer who'd been playing mind games with them all this time? The choice should've been easy, right? Slipping her uninjured hand into his, she let him pull her and her go bag from the vehicle. "What did you do?"

"Nothing big. Just convinced the people who bought the place from you to sell it to me." Carson led her up the driveway, slower than he wanted to go but fully aware of her limitations after surviving what she had.

Disbelief and something along the lines of joy etched into her features. Ivy couldn't seem to take her eyes off of the house. "When did you do this?"

"While you were recovering in the hospital. Not sure you know this, but you were asleep for a long time." A move of this magnitude had taken precision planning and people skills. But, in the end, he knew it was worth the effort. Just for the look on her face. "I know you had to give this house up when I went undercover. We couldn't hold on to our old lives when we started this war, but considering our options are limited to using *Sangre por Sangre* resources or putting you in the cross-hairs with a Socorro safe house, I figured this would be the best place to lie low for a couple days."

"How...? How is this possible?" she asked.

Carson offered her the key. "Want to go inside?"

She nodded, seemingly incapable of responding. They moved as one up the rest of the driveway and past the black iron gate protecting the front door from solicitors and anyone else looking for their pound of flesh. Ivy slid the key into the dead bolt and turned.

Max pushed past both of them, nearly knocking Carson off-balance. Her nails clicked against the simple, oversize tile installed throughout the entryway as she raced through the maze of rooms. The rug positioned to greet visitors crumpled behind her.

"Knock it off! You're going to break something." Carson guided his partner over the threshold, and for a moment, he couldn't help but think of the night Ivy had invited him inside this place for the first time. How she'd kissed him right here at the front door. It had been a simpler time then. All they'd had to contend with was the FBI's rules on office romances. Everything had gotten so...out of order since then.

"It all still looks the same." Ivy unwound her hand from his and limped down the narrow hall leading to the rest of the house. "What did you do, ask the previous owners to leave their furniture and belongings and get out?"

"Something like that." A lot like that actually. Though he'd certainly made it worth their while. Hundreds of thousands of dollars over value. The thing about working for criminals for so long was he'd learned to become one. He'd known his days as Dominic Rojas would have to come to an end eventually. He hadn't known the exact moment when, but Ivy's influence had trained him to prepare for every threat. Every possibility. The cartel wouldn't get the drop on him. No matter the circumstance, and so Carson had ensured his own future. With the help of *Sangre por Sangre*. He set Ivy's belongings by the door and followed after her into the kitchen. "It's purchased under another alias for obvious reasons. Your operative who works your team's security—Scarlett— helped with the details."

Ivy ran her uninjured hand the length of the expansive kitchen island. Large enough to seat four people, though Carson had never known his partner to invite anyone into the space but him. The tension drained from her shoulders minute by minute. "I didn't think I would ever get to be inside this place again. I drive by it sometimes. Wasn't too happy with them painting the garage a different color, but they took good care of it, from what I can see." She surveyed the kitchen and the attached living room. "Do you think there's a chance they left anything to eat?"

"Already on it." Carson dodged Max's beeline for the living room couch. "If you don't calm down, I'm going to put you outside."

Ivy's laugh followed her into the living room, where she sat down on the sofa beside the German shepherd, and in that moment, it was easy to imagine they were on the other side of this investigation. That they'd survived *Sangre por Sangre* and Sebastian and everything else the world threw at them, and all that was left was… this. This peace.

It had been so long since he'd allowed himself to relax, he wasn't sure he knew how to anymore, but right now, here with Ivy, he saw their future. A future he'd killed for, had nearly died for and sacrificed for.

In an instant, guilt—thick and hot and acidic— burned in his gut, eating away at his stomach lining. He'd built a life within the cartel. Dedicated himself to protecting the people he served with. They'd become his team at a time when he'd needed them the most.

But choosing Ivy meant abandoning them. Delivering them up to the slaughter when Socorro brought down the final judgment.

His fellow soldiers. The people he'd laughed with around bonfires in the middle of the desert while they waited for their next orders. Who'd pressed their backs against his in the middle of a firefight with the DEA. Who'd stood watch over him so he could grab a couple of hours of sleep out in the open. For the first time since he'd lost his mother he'd had a family of his very own.

Sebastian had been included in that group. Now there wasn't anything Carson wouldn't do to keep him from putting his hands on Ivy again, but his insides still raged as the two lives he'd created battled for dominance. "I'll see what I can scrounge up for food."

He set to work on inventorying the cabinets. Lucky for him, the previous owners had left a good amount behind. While he'd never been anything but a ramen chef as an FBI agent, there were some skills he'd been forced to rely on within the cartel. Being able to create a densely nutritional meal out of few ingredients, for one. Within minutes, Carson plated a sizable helping of homemade macaroni and cheese complete with hot dogs and brought two plates to the couch.

Max eyed him scornfully as he handed off Ivy's plate.

"Yours is in the kitchen. Try not to make a mess," he said.

The K-9 took that as permission to fly off the couch and skid across the tile floor. Only she failed to stop in time, crashing into the lower cabinets.

Ivy's laugh interrupted her initial bite, and she had to cover her mouth to keep the macaroni from falling back onto the plate. "Happy to see she's held on to some of that puppy excitement. It's nice, knowing she's still the same troublemaker I brought home so long ago. I missed that."

He had to remember that. That as much as Carson had missed of the real world over the past two years surviving and thriving within a drug cartel, Ivy had missed a lot, too.

"You should see her when I manage to get my hands on those special chips you used to eat." He took his first bite, and his entire body clung on to that single influx of calories as though he'd gone weeks without food rather than twelve hours. "You think she's hyper now. She practically flies on that stuff."

"Salt-and-vinegar chips aren't special." Ivy took another bite and seemingly melted as quickly as the cheese. "Kind of a delicacy for a cartel soldier. Apart from the fact the one time I offered you one, you threw it into the neighbor's backyard. I think you said something like vinegar isn't meant to be consumed."

"Yeah, well." He couldn't help but smile at the memory. A sliver of time when they'd been allowed to be nothing but themselves. "I might have changed my mind a little."

"Good to know." She speared her next bite of macaroni onto her fork, only didn't bring it to her mouth. In fact, Ivy let the fork skid along the outside of the plate. "Is there anything else you might've changed your mind on I should know about?"

"Yeah. There is." Carson set his unfinished plate on the coffee table. He'd been putting this off long enough. Unwilling to let go. But there was no future for him in the cartel. Not anymore. "I'm ready to come home."

Chapter Ten

Carson rolled into her from the other side of the bed, jarring her back into the present.

She'd been awake for hours. Replaying Sebastian's claims. That he'd killed Dr. Piel and those other women, that he'd been biding his time, proud of himself for taking up so much of her life. Every cell in her body wanted to live in denial, but none of it did his victims a bit of good. And that was all that mattered. The victims.

Ivy turned her attention to Carson. It hadn't mattered before, but she needed to know. Had Dr. Piel been involved with *Sangre por Sangre*, or had Sebastian used Socorro's physician as bait? To lure Ivy out into the open. To take someone she cared about away. To hurt her. The last few seconds before she'd collapsed into unconsciousness played at the edges of her mind. Of seeing Carson in the middle of the warehouse. Of not knowing which side he would choose in the face of her death. Would he have gone back to the cartel given the chance? Or had he meant what he'd said earlier about coming home?

Her mind was playing tricks on her again. Trying to create a threat when she was positive one wasn't there. It did the same thing every night, keeping her awake for hours. Imagining scenarios in which everything she loved was taken from her. Where the Pentagon refused to re-up Socorro's contract, leaving her team ungrounded and scattered. And where she learned of Carson's death. Two years was a long time to give her anxiety the playground it needed to thrive. But, at the same time, had prepared her for the worst.

There was no way she was going to be able to sleep tonight. Dr. Cavill's orders to get as much rest as possible could go to hell. Ivy slipped from the bed she and Carson shared, careful not to wake the mound of fur at the end. Her go bag had supplied everything she'd needed to survive for up to two weeks, but somehow she'd forgotten to pack something to sleep in. As though she'd tried to convince herself that survival didn't require sleep. Instead, she'd taken one of Carson's extra T-shirts. It was too big and drapey and exactly what she'd needed. Something comfortable that didn't scratch at the dozens of bandages keeping her from falling to pieces.

She tiptoed to the bedroom door, looking back to ensure she hadn't woken either Carson or Max. And froze. She'd come close to losing them back in that warehouse. She never wanted to feel that way again.

Ivy navigated through her old house as easily as she had done years ago. Muscle memory. This place... It had been her safe haven. Not just a house. She'd come to think of it as home. The first place she felt comfortable enough to be herself, to let go of the hurt and the pain and the defenses she'd weaponized on the job.

Something entirely hers. Not connected to her past or her origin. Though there were times when those memories penetrated these walls, they didn't have as much hold on her as they had back then. This was where she'd become her own person. Separate from the trauma and abuse and sexism.

It hadn't been until Carson signed on as her partner that she'd imagined this home as anything more than her own personal barricade against the world. It had become something more. He'd somehow maneuvered his way into her life and made himself at home. As though he'd always belonged here, and, in a way, he had. He'd even made it easy. And when she'd brought Max home to meet him, it had felt like they'd become a family of her own creation. A team.

But when he'd accepted the assignment to go undercover within *Sangre por Sangre*, everything had changed. She'd no longer had the option to fantasize about the future. She had to give all that up in an attempt to keep him alive.

Ivy couldn't help but run her fingers the length of the hallway as she headed toward the kitchen. This home was supposed to be theirs when the time was right, but that didn't feel possible anymore. She spotted her go bag by the door where Carson had left it and dragged it to the kitchen counter. He'd made it clear she couldn't contact her team or use any of the devices registered in her name, but she wasn't going to sever herself from the intel she needed either. "Thank goodness for VPNs."

Her operatives were equipped to handle any situation, including disappearing off the grid. While she preferred to use the resources available, she couldn't risk bringing the cartel down on Carson and Max. Ivy unpacked a clean laptop, formatted and wiped thanks to her security operative for situations just like this. The subscription and credit card she'd registered the VPN under was set to an alias she'd used while in the FBI. Still active the last time she'd checked. The payments were made through an endless loop of shell corporations set up to keep anyone trying to track her going in circles. To give her the time she needed to drop off the radar. Just in case.

"Show me what you've got." Ivy took a seat at the kitchen counter and logged in to her Socorro email. Hundreds of unread messages filled the queue. But she was only looking for one. "Bingo."

She tapped the bolded message from Chief Halsey. Incident report: 914 NM-516, Aztec, New Mexico.

Followed up on your statement. Partnered with Aztec PD to raid the salvage yard. Suspect has not been located. See report attached.

Halsey had always been a man of few words. Maybe that was why she'd always liked him. His significant other, Jocelyn, was the complete opposite. Always offering a baked good in hopes of getting people to open up. They were perfect for each other.

The Alpine Valley chief of police would've had to pull a good amount of strings to get his hands on the incident report from another jurisdiction, but she couldn't think about how she'd repay him right now. Opening the email, she scanned the first page of the file before moving on to the crime scene photos.

Yellow tents punctured through the whitewash of spotlights directing investigators to evidence. A saw blade tipped in blood, a stain directly below a hook mounted to the ceiling in the back office. A wrench angled diagonally across the floor twisted with dark hair.

Every image resurrected the pain in her side, but she moved on, forcing herself to take it all in. To relive the hours that would haunt her nightmares for years. There had to be something. Something to tell her who Sebastian really was. Blood, sweat, hair, fingerprints, cell phone GPS. It was impossible to interact with an environment and leave nothing behind. Especially given the advancements in forensics and technology.

She made a mental note to have Alpine Valley PD look into the Sensorvault data during the duration of her and Carson's stay inside the warehouse. If Sebastian had a cell phone on him, the largest collection of phone GPS in the world would register the number. Possibly even locate it. "Come on. Give me something I don't know."

"Still talking to yourself?" Carson's voice hitched her heart rate higher. He turned on the lights, coming into the kitchen. "You know that's considered a red flag, right? I bet your Socorro psychologist would be very interested to hear about it."

The onslaught to her vision receded after a few moments but broke her concentration. "The FBI didn't seem to think it was a problem, and my current boss doesn't give a crap. She just wants results. And Socorro doesn't employ a psychologist."

Which felt like an oversight on her part right then. Her operatives had come close to death, each and every single one of them, and while she believed in the power of love and finding their significant others to share that burden, love wasn't always a solution.

"The FBI didn't know about it. And your current boss is you." He moved into the kitchen, opening the first cabinet. Only he didn't seem to find what he was looking for. He continued on to the next and grabbed a glass from the shelf. "Still not sure how you were able to pass the psych eval after everything you've experienced."

"Compartmentalization is a superpower." She was only half invested in this back-and-forth they'd always had together. It had become something of a habit in the course of their partnership, but her attention was almost entirely focused on getting through Aztec PD's crime scene photos.

"And is running off no sleep a superpower?" He filled his glass with water from the fridge and took a drink. "You were stabbed less than forty-eight hours ago, Ivy. You lost a lot of blood. When are you going to give your body a chance to slow down and heal?"

"As much as I appreciate your concern, it's actually none of your concern." Her own words pulled her out of the flow state she'd sunk into while studying the photos, and Ivy regretted them instantly.

Carson stepped back as though he'd been sucker punched. He stared down into his glass, and she couldn't help but wonder if he was wishing he hadn't come out here at all. "And here I thought we were still partners who gave a crap about each other. Has that changed?"

"We are. I do. I'm sorry. I just…" Ivy tore her attention from the computer. Because this…they were important. "I didn't mean that the way that sounded. Of course I give a crap about you."

"And yet you're not convinced you're worth giving a crap about." The accusation hit harder than it should. "Do you know why I asked to be your partner all those years ago?"

That information caught her by surprise. "I wasn't aware you had a choice."

"I did. Your former partners, none of them wanted to work with you anymore. They saw you as a wild card who would do anything to close a case. No matter who you had to bulldoze in the process. You were difficult to work with, too blunt, too brash, too intense. Yeah, you closed more cases than anyone in our office, but it was at the expense of being one of the team." Carson set his water glass on the counter. "I saw an agent who needed to know she wasn't alone. That she had someone she could rely on, someone she could trust. I've tried to be that person for you, Ivy, but you're still operating as though you're the only one who can finish this mission."

She didn't know what to say to that, what to think. Except the truth. "I've always felt better alone. Because then no one could hurt me."

"Do you really think, after everything we've been through, that I would hurt you?" he asked.

"Everyone is capable of hurting the people they care

about." Ivy let her gaze drift back to the computer. And she froze. Her brain latched on to the photo within a photo on the screen. "What the hell?"

Carson penetrated into her peripheral vision, coming around to get a better look. "What is this?"

"Crime scene photos. Of the salvage yard. It's a long story." She pointed to the burned remnants of paperwork and photos captured by Aztec PD. "Look at this. Where is this?"

"I don't know. I didn't come across a room like that," he said. "It looks like an office."

"It's not the room I was hung upside down in. This is someplace new." She tried to enlarge the photo, but there was only so much her laptop could process.

"So?" Carson didn't see what she saw. Not yet.

"So, look at this partially burned photograph. Sebastian didn't burn the entire thing before leaving it behind." Dread spilled into her gut. Ivy shoved away from the counter and tipped her go bag upside down. She grabbed for the burner cell stuffed deep inside and punched in one of the numbers she'd memorized in case of emergency. Like now. "I've seen it before."

"What am I missing?" Agitation tensed his shoulders.

"Dr. Piel wasn't involved with *Sangre por Sangre* like we originally believed." The phone rang. Once. Twice. Three times. Voicemail kicked in. *Hey, it's Jocelyn. Leave your—* Ivy hung up and dialed again. No answer. "I think she was just the first target."

"CAN YOU MAKE this thing go any faster?" Ivy held on to the handle above the passenger-side door as they raced into Alpine Valley. She'd tried calling her logistics co-ordinator, Jocelyn Carville, a dozen times without any answer.

Alpine Valley's chief of police wasn't answering either.

Carson floored the accelerator. Dirt gusted across the unpaved road in front of them, blocking out his view of the lights up ahead. Months ago an entire cliffside had buried Alpine Valley after a bitter chief of police attempted to bring down *Sangre por Sangre* himself. Even before that, the cartel had raided secluded towns like this, burning everything in its path.

Now a killer could be loose in Alpine Valley's streets.

The engine revved higher at his touch, and the SUV bolted forward. "Try the police chief again."

Ivy allowed herself a moment of unbalance and grabbed for her phone with her uninjured hand. She wasn't supposed to be here. Her physician had specifically instructed her to rest, but trying to talk her out of helping one of her fellow operatives had been out of the question. She raised the phone to her ear. And waited. "No voicemail. It just keeps ringing. It's like his phone is turned off. That's not like Baker. He's never been out of reach."

Carson didn't want to offer theories as to why Alpine Valley's chief of police suddenly wasn't available. No good came of catastrophizing. But there was a chance Sebastian or someone within the cartel had gotten to the chief and his Socorro partner first. There was no other reason why a photo of Jocelyn should've been in that warehouse office. "This isn't your fault, Ivy. You didn't bring this down on them."

"That's easy to say when you aren't the one who is supposed to protect them." She inhaled audibly. "My operatives—my team—have been there from day one. They believe in the cause just the same as I do, if not more. They're the ones who are in the field. They're the ones getting shot and stabbed and abducted. Because I pay them to. They risk their lives and the lives of the people they love because of me, and it's up to me to make sure they make it out of this alive."

Carson checked the rearview mirror, targeting Max lying across the back seat. The K-9 locked her gaze on him. "Max has been undercover with me since the day I was recruited by Sebastian. It was a risk bringing her with me, especially as young as she was, but I knew I needed the extra protection. I didn't have anyone else as long as I was part of the cartel. She's risked her life for me more times than I can count. Not because I asked her to. But because she loves me. Those operatives you have working for you, Ivy, they're not just doing a job because you give them a paycheck in return. They believe in you. They trust you. They would've found a job that doesn't get them shot and stabbed otherwise."

She was quiet for a moment. "Should you get the chance to meet my team, I don't recommend you tell them you just compared them to a German shepherd. It might not go over well."

He couldn't help but smile at that, at her willingness to add a bit of humor to a terrifying situation. Carson set his hand on her knee and squeezed. "It's going to be okay. I promise."

"I'm not sure that's something you can promise, Carson." Ivy faced him, the dim glow of the SUV's control panel washing her in a blue tint. "We don't even know what we're walking into."

"It doesn't matter." He didn't know how to explain his own brand of confidence right there in that moment. "Because we're walking in there together."

Carson followed the navigation mounted between them, taking a hard right onto Alpine Valley's Main Street. Evidence that the cartel had left its mark was everywhere, in half-burned buildings, new construction, and shaded windows this late at night.

"Up on the left." Ivy was already peeling herself out of her seat by the time he came to a full stop in front of the modest rambler coated in a dark stucco. The house itself stuck out among the ones on either side of it with their traditional Mexican style and coloring, making it an easy target. She unholstered her weapon with her nondominant hand, but not as awkwardly as he'd assumed she would. Which meant she'd practiced shooting with both hands. Always ready for the next threat. "No lights on inside or vehicles on the streets. Do you see any movement around the perimeter?"

Carson shoved the SUV into Park, getting Max's attention. She perked up in the back seat, then scanned her surroundings out the window. Ready. "No. Nothing."

Still, something didn't feel right. It was the same sensation of dread he'd experienced inside the salvage yard.

He pulled his backup sidearm and checked the rounds left in the magazine. "We go in together. You go where I go. Understand?"

The last time they'd entered into a house with cartel inside, Ivy had ended up under the killer's control, and it had taken Carson losing another kidney to get her back. He couldn't go through that again.

"I understand." No argument this time. No trying to take control of the situation. She was trusting him to put her operative and the chief of police at the top of his priority list. "They have a German shepherd. Maverick. He's a bomb detection K-9 and fiercely protective of Jocelyn."

"In that case, we'll let Max go first." Except Carson didn't want to leave the safety of the vehicle. No. It wasn't that. He'd gone headfirst into any number of situations with higher stakes. He didn't want Ivy to leave the safety of the vehicle. But asking her to stay behind would betray their partnership, and he couldn't turn back on his decision to come home now. Not when he was so close to getting the future he'd always wanted. "On three."

"Three." Ivy didn't wait for the countdown. Every second they hesitated could cost her teammate, and she was the kind of person to take mistakes personally.

So Carson followed. He let Max out of the back seat, approaching the front door low and fast. Ivy moved in time with him despite her injuries. Whether by force or by habit, he wasn't sure. They reached the front door, but Carson was the one to pull back the heavy metal screen protecting the aged wood. It was a recent installation. Considering the nature of the couple's work, he was willing to bet the Socorro operative had added the extra measure of security. "Does your logistics coordinator have a Socorro security system, too?"

"No. Baker wouldn't allow it. He doesn't particularly agree with our values, but I imagine he's got his own security system in place." Ivy stood back enough to give him room to swing the screen door wide and test the doorknob.

The dead bolt hadn't been engaged.

"Is he the kind that dares criminals to break into his home, or was this supposed to be locked?" Carson tried to make out a layout of the home with his limited vision, but the only way to get a read on the place was to step inside.

Ivy raised her weapon, taking the first step over the threshold. She led him straight into the living room with a hallway branching directly to the back of the house and what he assumed was the kitchen. Another branch went right. Most likely to the bedrooms. She scanned the living room gun first and allowed his nerves to take a step down. "Clear."

He moved in behind her, then pushed ahead down the hallway. Max beat him to it, her tags tinkling together as she advanced. The kitchen was small and looked to be original, from what little he could see of the streetlights coming through the windows. No movement. No one waiting to ambush them. "Clear."

They turned their attention to the hallway. "I'm thinking nobody is here, or Maverick isn't a very good guard dog."

Ivy didn't answer, seemingly bracing herself as she

moved into the hallway. The first bedroom housed an office. It belonged to the chief, from the disarray of paperwork on the surface of the desk. No logistics co-ordinator would be so careless. The room straight across from it looked to be a guest bedroom. Made up nice and tidy. Small bathroom with no windows midway through. A heavy metal garage door on the other side. Locked.

Two bedrooms sat at the end of the hall, almost making a T formation. Ivy took the one on the right. Carson the one on the left. He kicked the door inward. But the door stopped short of hitting the wall behind it. He hit the light switch near the door.

And found a body.

"Son of a bitch." Holstering his weapon, Carson dropped to both knees and flipped the uniformed officer onto his back. Blood leaked from a head wound most likely caused by someone bashing his head in from behind. The man's phone lay in pieces beside him. Would explain why Ivy's calls never made it through. "I'm guessing this is the chief you're looking for?"

Ivy abandoned her search. "Baker. Damn it."

"He's alive." Carson almost lost himself in the relief at the feel of the chief's pulse against his first two fingers. Broken skin and blood across the officer's knuckles told a good story. "Busted up, from what I can see. Man put up a fight. Whoever was on the other end isn't going to get far."

More details came into view as Max bounded for another body across the room. Only this one wasn't human. She sniffed at the unconscious German shepherd in concern.

The chief's groan filled the room. Baker Halsey blinked

at Carson a few times before some deep-rooted pain no one could see set in. Alpine Valley's elected hero pushed his upper body off the floor. "Please tell me you're here to get the recipe of Jocelyn's famous chocolate chip cookies."

"Chief, you were attacked," Ivy said. "Did you see by who?"

"No. Sons of bitches caught me from behind. Must've been waiting behind the front door when I got home." He set sights on the K-9 still unmoving a few feet away. Chief Halsey practically crawled to the dog and brought the German shepherd into his lap. "I got you, bud. Hell, Jocelyn's going to murder me for letting them touch Maverick. Where is she?"

"She wasn't with you?" Carson asked.

"What? No. I just got off shift. I came home. The house was dark, but I saw Maverick…" Fear contorted the chief's face, and he maneuvered Maverick off his lap. Baker shoved to stand—unbalanced and grabbing for the nearest wall. Carson moved to assist but was rejected. "Jocelyn never goes anywhere without Maverick. They're a team. Ivy, where the hell is my partner?"

Chief Halsey didn't wait for an answer. He shoved into the hallway. "Jocelyn!"

"We've already searched the house. She isn't here." Ivy tried to keep up with the chief of police. In vain. The man was on a mission, the same kind of mission that had held Carson in its grip in that damn warehouse: getting to the woman he loved. "Baker, think. What can you remember up until you blacked out?"

"Jocelyn!" Baker flipped on every light in the place. The chief was reaching for his weapon, but the holster on his hip was empty. Whoever had attacked him had stripped him of his weapons. The man was close to losing it. He threaded both hands into his hair. "All right. Give me a minute. The sliding glass door. It was open when I came home. I thought something was off. We never go out there."

Ivy bolted for the kitchen and out the back door.

"Stay here, Chief." There was no telling what they would find. Carson followed Ivy into the backyard.

"Go to hell," Baker said. "That's my partner."

The motion-sensor spotlights lit up.

Exposing the woman left for dead in the middle of the yard.

Chapter Eleven

"He's targeting us one by one." Ivy couldn't forget the images of Jocelyn as she'd lain there. Left in the middle of her own yard. The message gouged into her back was the same as the one found on Dr. Piel.

There's no escaping Sangre por Sangre.

Except Jocelyn had somehow survived. EMTs had managed to get a breathing tube down the logistics coordinator's throat in time. Ivy's operative was recovering in the hospital with Chief Halsey and Maverick refusing to leave her side. The dog had been taken down with a sedative but would make a full recovery.

It had been too close.

Too personal.

Ivy stared out the wall of windows in her office. The weight of her team's attention pressed between her shoulder blades. She was supposed to keep things like this from happening. She'd been responsible for training them, for getting them through the hard assignments and out onto the other side. Now two of her operatives had been attacked, with one of them dead.

"I've sent Elena and the baby to her parents' house." Cash Meyers, Socorro's forward scout, prided himself on seeing the threat from a distance, on knowing when an attack was coming. But there was no way for him to see this. His new family had been put at risk. Because of her.

This threat had come directly from Ivy's past. Something she'd never shared with any of them. She'd never seen any value in being anything more than their fearless leader. Who would follow her if they knew she couldn't face the nightmares she'd created, let alone send them out into the field to confront new ones? She faced what was left of her team and, in that moment, felt considerably under-experienced in finishing what she'd started two years ago.

Carson stood in the corner of her office, so out of place, and yet necessary. To this mission. To Socorro. To her. He hadn't contributed to the discussion, and the truth was, she hadn't expected him to. It was easy to imagine him shouldering the responsibility of what had happened, just as she had. Being crushed underneath it. The only way they'd get through this was together. He'd said that. "What about Maggie, Jones? Have you been able to get any information?"

Jones Driscoll—Socorro's combat coordinator— wouldn't take an attack on this team lying down. He'd risked his life to pull a war correspondent out from the cartel's grip without hesitation and brought down a corrupt senator in the process. Of every operative she employed, he would be the one to burn everything to the ground. And maybe that was exactly what she needed now. "We thought *Sangre por Sangre* had gone to ground before—the entire organization is a ghost now. No chatter. No corner deals on the streets. I've been monitoring the smuggling routes, but all I found was a bunch of abandoned trucks with product still inside. The cartel's been forced to cut back on operations over the past few months. Now it's like they've given up entirely. Maggie reached out to a couple of her contacts, but all she's managed to uncover is a couple of low-level soldiers who don't know what the hell is going on. We've got them in one of the holding cells downstairs, but they're not talking. Whoever killed those women and attacked Jocelyn is staying to the shadows. Feels like he's waiting for something."

"Not waiting. He's compartmentalizing." Carson unfolded his arms and raised his chin. Confident and ready to take charge. Ivy needed a bit of that right now. "There are protocols the cartel follows when it's in danger. First, consolidate information. The fewer people who know of his plan, the less chances there are of a betrayal. Sebastian will only trust the people he's known since he joined the cartel twenty years ago. Next, he'll take an account of *Sangre por Sangre*'s assets. Safe houses, cash, product and alliances. The cartel hasn't had any luck attacking Socorro directly. Picking us off one by one is his only option, but he won't do it slowly."

"And you know all of this how? Who are you?" Granger Morais's graveled advice had been Ivy's voice of reason from the beginning. The former Department of Defense counterterrorism agent was the first operative she'd recruited, and he in turn had brought Socorro's security consultant on board. He pushed for the logical decision in every scenario, questioning every turn and vetting every fact. Without him, Ivy wouldn't have come this far.

"You don't recognize him?" Scarlett Beam—Socorro's security expert—studied Carson from head to toe. Her fiery red hair only gave a glimpse of the wild card underneath. Scarlett was the type of operative to make her own rules while still getting the job done and protecting the people she cared about. Her DEA partner and his son could attest to that after Scarlett had managed to uncover a massive shipment of cartel fentanyl and somehow managed to bring the boy home alive. She genuinely worked to protect and defend, and she took the safety of this team personally. "You're in the presence of our very own undercover source within the cartel. The guy who's been giving us all the good info on *Sangre por Sangre*'s lieutenants, shipments, targets and assets to hit."

"This is Carson Lang, though some of you may know him as Dominic Rojas. He's been vital to neutralizing the *Sangre por Sangre* threat for the past two years," Ivy said.

Except Carson was more than a tool Socorro had used to its advantage. He was Ivy's partner. The man who'd saved her life. Twice. Who'd sacrificed everything he'd known and loved, to protect her and bring a killer to justice. He was passionate for their cause, carrying around a heavy heart that had lost too much over the years. A misfit who'd never really adapted to anyone except the chosen few he allowed into his life. He was creative and isolating and seemingly stuck in a never-ending cycle of loss.

And she loved every facet of him. Would give up this entire company if asked to keep him in her life. Because they belonged together. They were partners.

Granger seemed to grow in size as he crossed Ivy's office and closed the distance between him and Carson. Max shook herself out of a deep sleep and got to her feet in response. At the ready for a confrontation. "You're the one who told us the cartel was targeting Charlie Acker and using her extremist family to strike the state capitol building last month."

"Yes," Carson said.

The counterterrorism agent extended his hand. "Thank you. For saving her life. If it weren't for you, I wouldn't have made it to Charlie in time."

The men shook, and an air of agreement wove through the office.

"Aah, I can feel the love." Scarlett leaned back in her chair, smile wide. Pulling her phone, she skimmed her finger across the screen and raised the device. "Now hug. I want it for the company newsletter."

"I will kill you and your little dogs, too." Granger shot her a look that would send any cartel soldier running for cover, but it had no effect on this team. They were all well aware of when an empty threat wasn't so empty.

"Good luck." Scarlett snapped a photo and sat back in her chair. "I'm teaching the twins some new commands. Primarily how to break into locked rooms. You'll never hear them coming, Granger."

"As much as I hate to break up...whatever is happening here, we need a plan," Jones said. "I don't know about any of you, but I'm not willing to sit back and let these sons of bitches pick us off. What's the move, boss?"

The team looked to Ivy.

And she…looked to Carson. For a little bit of that confidence and maybe some assurance. She'd built this company from the ground up. She'd battled against corrupt congressmen and Pentagon officials. She'd coordinated with local law enforcement, her old FBI office and the DEA on assignments. There wasn't a single battle she wasn't willing to take on alone. And yet, right then, she felt the need to rely on him.

The shift rocked through her. Because he'd been right: she didn't have to do this alone. Not anymore. Maybe she never had. She had an entire team willing and waiting to fight this war alongside her. But constantly living on the edge of survival had left her feeling isolated. Convinced her threats were everywhere even when there weren't any, lied to her about who she could trust. Carson had seen through all of it. He always had.

"The man we know as Sebastian seems to hold a good amount of power within *Sangre por Sangre*." Ivy filled her lungs to the point of stretching the stitches in her side. "He's made connections and most likely built a few of his own he'll be calling on to come after us individually. We're not going to let that happen."

She steepled her fingers on the surface of her desk, looking at each one of her operatives in turn. "We've been fighting this war through small assignments and conflicts up to this point. We've been shot and stabbed and tortured for information. There have been broken bones and explosions and entire buildings coming down on top of us. Our loved ones have suffered. We've lost team members and people close to us. We've watched entire lives be destroyed by the cartel. Homes gone, towns buried underneath mudslides, families ripped apart. Our K-9s have stood by our sides, risking their lives to please us. All of that has led us here. To the end of the line."

She set her sights on Carson. "I'm not going to pretend I'm not responsible for what's happening now. This killer is targeting each and every one of you to hurt me. To force me to watch as I lose everyone and everything I care about because I have declared war on the cartel. He won't stop until he's put every one of us in the ground and burned this building to the ground. So I'll give you a choice."

Ivy held herself a little taller. "You can walk away. All of you. You can go home, be with your families. I will write you references for your next job, and I'll pay your severance for your service to this company and to me. I'll provide new identities, if that's what you require, and there will be no hard feelings. But I'm realizing now I can't do this alone. I need you at my side. All of you. I need my team. Will you help me?"

Silence ate into her nerves as she dared study her operatives for a reaction. Seconds ticked off, excruciating and hard to swallow.

Until Scarlett shoved to her feet. "Looks like Hans and Gruber will get to test out those new commands we've been working on after all."

Jones stood. "It's about time we finish this."

Granger nodded, sharp and curt. He was in.

Cash folded his arms across his chest. "I love seeing Bear take bites out of cartel soldiers. I'm in, whatever you need, boss."

Ivy turned to Carson. The same speech applied to him. He could walk away from this. From her. No hard feelings. She would acquire a new identity from her contacts at the Pentagon and pay him the severance he'd risked his life for. But a large part of her needed him more than anyone else on this team.

Carson pulled his phone from his pocket and headed for her office door. "I've got to make a call."

CARSON PICKED UP his pace toward the elevators.

The call was a ploy. To get out of that room. Away from Ivy's team. Honestly, he had no idea where the hell he was going, but one of the operatives had said the cartel soldiers they'd brought into custody were being held downstairs. He'd find them sooner or later.

He hit the elevator's down button with a little too much force and stepped back. Max caught up without so much as a huff. As though she was as disappointed in him as much as he was with himself.

Movement registered in the reflective stainless steel, and he turned to find Ivy standing there. She'd changed back into her slacks and blazer, washed her hair, scrubbed the dirt and blood from her skin. The woman he'd pulled out of that warehouse was buried beneath the armor she'd built for herself over the past two years. Never to surface again as long as she could help it. "Tell me what's going through your head."

He didn't want to have this conversation. Not yet. Not here. Carson hit the elevator call button a second time, but the damn thing wouldn't speed the hell up. "You did a good job rallying the troops in there. I can see why they've stayed on with Socorro as long as they have. You should start working on your strategy to track down Sebastian. Every second counts."

"And what will you be doing?" The fabric of her slacks rustled as she moved in close, and a flare of heat shot up his neck.

It spread down his spine and wrapped around his rib cage, squeezing him in some invisible vise. "There's something I need to take care of."

"Would it have anything to do with the two cartel soldiers Jones brought in?" she asked.

He didn't want to lie to her. She deserved better than that. The elevator arrived, doors parting, and Carson took a step into the car. Max followed, planting her butt at his feet.

Except Ivy was right behind him. She threaded her arm between the doors and prevented them from closing. "Just tell me what's going on, Carson. After everything we've been through the past few days, everything we've promised one another, you at least owe me that."

She was right. Of course she was right. That same sinking feeling he'd experienced before Sebastian had betrayed him at the salvage yard took hold. He was standing on the edge of a blade. Tip too far in one direction, make one choice, and he lost the family he'd found within the cartel. Tip too far in the other, and he lost Ivy. His cartel world and his personal world were mutually exclusive. He couldn't have one without losing the other. The idea of helping Socorro slaughter and arrest the soldiers—the people—he'd come to know and rely on surged acid into his throat. There were good people in those ranks. Not just killers. People who'd had no other choice than to join the cartel to save their families, their friends, their way of life. At the same time, these were men and women he'd only known through becoming someone he wasn't, and choosing them over Ivy threatened to tear his heart in half. "I think you already know the answer you're looking for."

Color seemed to drain from her already-pale skin. Her mouth parted on a strong exhalation, but it was the only sign she'd filled in the blanks. Like always, she was trying to hold herself together, to keep anyone from seeing her vulnerabilities. "You're going back. To the cartel."

"I don't have a choice," he said. "There are people there who were just following orders, Ivy. They don't have anything to do with calling the shots. They weren't the ones who targeted Alpine Valley or retaliated for a missing fentanyl shipment. They were just trying to survive. Like me. They deserve a chance to get out while they still can."

"If by survive you mean kidnap an eight-year-old boy to force his sister to turn herself over to their lieutenant." Ivy's voice lost the confused quality it had taken a minute ago, growing stronger. Puncturing him like a thousand needles. "Or when they abducted and tortured a war correspondent because she witnessed the cartel slaughter ten American soldiers in the desert. How about when they put a bounty on an innocent woman's head because she refused to be connected to her extremist family of preppers? Was that your friends' way of surviving? Was it yours?"

She could list a dozen more incidents. With good reason. A chill spread along his back as he realized the position he'd put himself in. If he wasn't choosing Socorro—if he wasn't choosing Ivy—he was choosing to become her enemy. Black and white. No going back. "That's not the least bit fair, and you know it. I agreed to go undercover. We both knew what that would entail, what I would have to do to work my way up the ladder and gain the cartel's trust, but I don't expect you to understand what it means to be part of a team. All your former partners were right. You bulldoze anyone and everyone to get your way and solve a case, and I was fine with that for a long time. Because you provided justice to those who deserved it. You kept more people from getting hurt and you saved lives. But you're so blinded by one man's atrocities that you're not willing to see there might be more innocent lives involved in this investigation than the ones you found in the desert."

Silence built between them. Heavy and thick and unrelenting.

Ivy stepped over the threshold into the elevator, her heels on the verge of getting caught in the tracks.

"I have watched the cartel tear apart people's lives. They've sold girls and women for profit. They've spread their drugs and killed children. They punished Dr. Piel and Jocelyn for simply having a connection to this company, and they'll continue killing my team unless I put a stop to it. Do you know what that tells me?" Ivy didn't let him answer. "That tells me that every single soldier, contracted killer, lieutenant and supplier is complicit in the cartel's actions. You talk about the low-level soldiers, these friends you made while undercover, as innocent? There are no innocents inside the *Sangre por Sangre* cartel, Carson, and I will not let any of them walk away without answering for their crimes."

"And that's why I have to leave," he said. "I have to give them a chance. Just one of them. Please."

She smoothed her expression, as though he were a stranger. "From the moment I found you in my safe house four nights ago, there was a part of me that wondered where your loyalties really fell. Your insistence on hiding out in a cartel safe house was just the start, but I think it was your connection to Sebastian and your willingness to consult with a cartel soldier on this investigation that gave you away. I convinced myself I was being paranoid, that there was no way my partner could've been turned, but all of that paranoia was with good reason. Because you're not my partner anymore."

His heart shot into his throat with denial. But Carson only let her words hang between them.

She dropped her hand away from the elevator door sensors and allowed the elevator to start closing. "You have two hours before Socorro comes for your organization, Dominic Rojas. I suggest you get the people you're trying to save as far from here as possible. Before you're caught in the fight."

The doors sealed between them.

Carson stared into his reflection as gravity shoved

his stomach higher in his torso. An emptiness he'd managed to keep a rein on grew bigger, as he added more distance between himself and Ivy.

Max moaned at his feet, echoing the hurt and the pain doubling inside his chest, but there was no going back for them. He'd made his choice, and Ivy had made hers. Neither of them was willing to consider the other's position, and everything he'd hoped for the future—for them—stayed behind in Ivy's office.

Second by second, the Carson Lang he'd been over these past few days slipped to the back of his mind. The elevator doors parted on the level below, and he stepped into a black-on-black corridor. Every inch the cartel soldier he'd trained himself to become. Within minutes, this building would become enemy territory. A maze meant to confuse and trap him and keep him from getting what he wanted. He had minutes to locate the two soldiers taken into custody and get out.

Carson's fingers tingled to unholster his weapon, but any threat inside the building was sure to alert the security system and the woman behind it. He and Max moved along the corridor with an abstract idea of how the building had been laid out, according to Ivy's and the other operatives' descriptions.

It was enough.

They made a right at the end of the main hallway, coming face-to-face with a wall of glass. Not so much a window. One-way glass that looked into a single interrogation room. Carson recognized the woman inside. Her dark hair had been braided back tight enough to pull at the frame of her face. She paced back and forth, stripped of her weapons. She'd never liked being put in a closed-off space with no exit. Always had a knack for finding the best way out of any given situation. It was one of the reasons he'd been able to get himself and Sebastian out of the cartel headquarters when the entire building had started coming down on them. She'd been the one to lead them out.

He went for the door and threw it open.

She turned on him. Every inch of her lean frame ready for a fight. Confusion creased her wide, heart-shaped face, and she backed off, lunging for the door. "Dominic? What the hell are you doing here?"

"Getting you out of here." He didn't wait for her response, moving on to the room next door. Carson threw the second door open, confronted with one of the younger recruits brought into the cartel within the past couple of months. The rookie didn't have a lot of know-how about how things worked yet, but he'd been willing to learn from the beginning. "Come on. We don't have a lot of time."

"How did you find us?" the first soldier asked. "How did you know we were here?"

"I've got my ways." They didn't have time for twenty questions. There was no telling if Ivy's two-hour head start would hold with the other operatives. They had to move. Right the hell now. "Do you want to get out of here, or do you want to wait to see what Socorro is going to do to you to get you to talk?"

"Right behind you." The second soldier added a hitch to his step, and the three of them and Max retraced Carson's steps. He hit the elevator call button, every cell in his body on fire considering the possibilities waiting for them downstairs.

But Ivy had kept her word.

Carson, Max and both cartel soldiers hit the parking garage, located an SUV with keys sitting in the front seat and sped out of the garage. Leaving Socorro—and Ivy—behind.

Chapter Twelve

"You're just going to let them leave?" Granger's logic wasn't going to help her right now.

"Carson made his choice." Ivy watched plumes of dirt kick up behind the SUV racing across the New Mexico desert. Her heart twisted hard every second it kept driving away. "Give them thirty minutes, then activate the GPS."

Though she already had an idea of where Carson and his fellow soldiers were headed. This final war between *Sangre por Sangre* and Socorro had practically been fated. She'd only let him leave because they could track him.

"Do you know what it took to capture those two?" Jones extended one hand toward the massive wall of windows, motioning to the retreating vehicle. "The woman nearly gutted me like a fish. I'm lucky to be alive, and you're just letting them leave?"

"Easy, tiger. The boss knows what she's doing." Scarlett's insistence on being the voice of reason didn't sit well. Socorro's security operative didn't usually agree with Ivy's strategy, which had led to the installation of a hundred pounds of C-4 lining every hallway in the building in the past in an effort to protect the team. It had worked. And also destroyed the garage during a cartel ambush a few months ago. Scarlett's calm demeanor made Ivy wonder what the woman had up her sleeve. "You gotta make them feel safe, give them a reason to let their guard down. Then when they least expect it, you trigger the explosive."

"Come again?" Granger asked. "Are you telling me you've wired our SUVs to explode? How far is the frequency?"

"Anywhere in the world. That's the beauty of satellites," Scarlett said. "Don't give me that look. The next time you or Charlie or any one of us is abducted, you'll be begging me for a kill switch. This way, we're prepared."

"Wait. Does King know about this?" Jones asked. "Does he let you drive his son around in an SUV wired with explosives?"

"I'm not allowed to drive Julien," the security consultant said. "But that's not connected to the C-4. No."

"Enough." Ivy couldn't deal with this right now. She swallowed to counteract the emotion clogging her throat since her final conversation with Carson. But, worse, the idea of coming face-to-face with him on opposite sides of the divide triggered a grief so intense she couldn't breathe. She'd trusted him. Counted on him. She'd...loved him, damn it.

They'd agreed how far they would go to see this through, and now... Now he was choosing the wrong side. He was choosing the enemy over her. Over their partnership. To make matters worse, he'd taken her dog in the process. Part of her was still in denial. She'd wanted him to turn back, to choose her over the mission. Wondered if she'd been right in letting him go, but if he was hell-bent on saving a few cartel soldiers, she'd at least use his exit to her advantage. "Jones, check in with the hospital. I want an update on Jocelyn's recovery. Get ahold of Chief Halsey if you have to, and let him know of our plans to initiate contact with *Sangre por Sangre*. Granger, contact the medical examiner and see if he has any more to add from Dr. Piel's autopsy. And, Scarlett, get those explosives off my SUVs before someone ends up hurting themselves."

"Yes, ma'am," Scarlett said. "But to be clear, it's not easy to trigger the explosives. There's a whole security code you have to put into the system to connect to the devices, and—"

"Thank you, Scarlett. That will be all." She just needed to be alone. To figure out what to do next. She'd given Carson a two-hour head start with the intention of providing him the opportunity to change his mind, but he'd called her bluff.

Movement registered behind her as the team headed for her office door. And her heart hurt, damn it. As though Carson had taken it between both hands and squeezed as hard as he could just to see what would happen. Air rushed from her lungs as the betrayal hooked into her. She was about to fall into a thousand shards of glass from the invisible pain.

"Boss." Granger's reflection took position behind her injured shoulder. Then Jones and Scarlett and Cash. "We're your team. Every single one of us has experienced loss and betrayal. Sometimes from the people we love the most. You don't have to hide from us. We've got your back. Whatever you need."

"I need..." She didn't know what she needed. A single tear escaped her control, and a rush of embarrassment flooded through her. Ivy immediately swiped it away as she turned to face them. The men and women who'd devoted themselves to carrying out her own personal crusade. Except two had been taken from their ranks. Jocelyn was recovering, but Dr. Piel would never step foot in this building again. "I need this to make sense, but no matter how I reframe it or pull it apart, it just doesn't."

"Which part of this war has made sense in the past two years, Ivy?" Cash asked. "*Sangre por Sangre* doesn't follow the rules. Because no cartel has gained this much power in the entire history of the drug epidemic. This is all new territory, for all of us. But we knew one day they would come for us. They've tried en masse in the past. Now it seems this Sebastian guy has figured out how to slide the blade in without us even noticing."

"Doesn't mean he gets to walk away in one piece," Jones said.

That hadn't been at all what she'd meant, but exposing her lack of judgment—her grief—wasn't in her DNA. Maybe that was the problem. She and Carson were supposed to be partners. Had made a commitment to one another. They'd started this war against the cartel together. Only now... He was gone. He'd been there when she'd needed him the most, but had she returned the investment? Had she been as committed to him as

Carson had been to her, or had she let her past dictate their relationship? Was her stepfather still finding ways to show her she wasn't strong enough—for this job, to finish what she started, to keep a partner—from beyond the grave?

Ivy wanted to deny that man had anything to do with the life she'd built for herself, that he'd encouraged her to rise above her trauma and finally take control. Except she couldn't. Every experience, every conversation, every fantasy and hope she'd had since the age of ten had made her into the woman standing in this office. Including the abuse she'd suffered at the hands of a parent who was supposed to protect her. She couldn't forget any of it, and that failure to disassociate from that part of her life had followed her into the most important relationship she'd ever had.

And cost her everything.

What that meant for the future, she didn't know. All she could do was focus on the next step. "Every battle between this team and the cartel has ended in one place."

"*Sangre por Sangre*'s headquarters." Granger folded his arms across his broad chest. "Hell, is there even anything left of that place? Charlie and I were nearly crushed to death when all of the new underground tunnels collapsed last month."

She remembered. Having been the one to pull him out of the collapse. "Check out the latest satellite images before disabling the explosives you installed on the fleet, Scarlett. If there's movement, we'll have a better idea of what we're up against."

"I can bring it up now." Scarlett took her phone out from her back pocket and tapped both thumbs against the screen in a nonsensical order to anyone but her. "I'm repositioning the Pentagon's satellite over the headquarter coordinates. Should take just a couple minutes."

Scarlett's phone chimed. "That's not good."

"That might be the worst response you could possibly come up with." Jones had never been one to hide his criticism of others, but there'd been less of it since he and Maggie had gotten involved in the past year.

"Is there a problem with the satellites?" Ivy asked.

"No. I was able to reposition them without any problems." Scarlett turned the phone to face Ivy. "This is the problem."

Ivy lost control of her exhalation and took the phone from the security operative. "When were these images taken?"

"Less than an hour ago." Scarlett looked to the men at her side. "Seems *Sangre por Sangre* isn't on its last legs as our intel suggested. There has to be at least a couple hundred vehicles parked around that building."

"It's Sebastian." Ivy didn't know where the theory had come from. She felt it as nothing more than an instinct that had been trying to warn her over the past four days. But now, staring at the screen, she'd never been more sure of anything in her life. She handed Scarlett's phone to Granger, who in turn tensed as though he'd watched someone kick his K-9.

"What do you mean, boss?" Cash took the phone next, refusing to allow his expression to give away the dread they were all feeling.

"There's no way a low-level cartel soldier would have been able to round up this many recruits in a matter of two days. Not as long as upper management was still in control and as sure as hell not just because of me or Carson." Energy she had no idea what to do with skittered through her as the pieces started falling into place. "This kind of power only comes from years of earning your subordinates' respect, of sending warnings and exacting punishment when orders aren't followed, and people try to get out."

Granger seemed to grow another two inches. "You're not saying—"

"We've been looking for the identity of *Sangre por Sangre*'s founder since we got into this mess. Carson was never able to get a face-to-face. Didn't even have a clue as to his whereabouts or his name. Lieutenants were handed orders through coded messages and delivery services. Everything was hands-off. Every soldier we've gotten to talk has only called him *el jefe*, and I think now we know why." She slapped her hand against the nearest window. The entire pane shook under the force, but it was nothing compared to the frustration burning through her now. "He was right there in front of his own soldiers the whole time. Pretending to be one of them, keeping an eye on them, making sure they did what they were told."

"You mean this Sebastian, the guy who attacked you at the salvage yard, is actually the leader of the cartel?" Scarlett asked.

"It's the only way this makes sense." Ivy was still trying to process this new possibility. Her mind was working faster than her mouth. "He killed those women to send a message. *No one escapes* Sangre por Sangre. But in the two years Carson has been undercover, no one was willing to offer information on a killer in the network who carved symbols into his victims' backs. Because they knew who was responsible and what would happen if they identified their leader."

"Wait." Cash stepped forward. "Then doesn't that mean this Sebastian would've had to have known that Carson was part of an undercover operation from the beginning? I mean, he couldn't identify the top brass for two years."

Acid pushed into her throat. Ivy raced for her cell phone and pressed the autodial to call Carson. Despite the lingering effects of their last conversation, she couldn't let him go through with this. "He's walking straight into a trap."

THIS PLACE WAS on the verge of total collapse.

Carson wasn't sure the structure could take much more.

The multistory building had been designed to hide in plain sight. Meant to bring the cartel together, to pool resources and serve as a headquarters as efficient and deadly as the very people trying to destroy *Sangre por Sangre*. But a handful of explosives had broken it down, eroded its foundation and turned it into something worthless.

Not entirely unlike the emptiness coiling through him.

"Get rid of the vehicle." He tossed the keys into the

back seat to the youngest of the soldiers and shoved free of the SUV. Knowing Ivy, he was sure she'd have equipped her fleet with GPS and possibly even better countermeasures. But she had promised him a two-hour head start. He trusted her to keep her word—for now—but her patience would run out sooner or later.

There was a small chance Sebastian had managed to contact upper management since their showdown in the salvage yard, but the way Carson had left him unconscious and bleeding would buy him the time he needed to defend his case. At least, that was the hope.

The soldier positioned behind him had caught the keys and gotten out, letting Max hop down from the back driver's-side door. In less than a minute, dirt kicked up behind the stolen vehicle but disappeared over the ridge of the man-made bowl acting as a defense system around the building. If anyone came close to this place, the cartel saw them coming. Especially now that upper management seemed to have called in every asset, soldier and resource on and off the books. "There a party I don't know about?"

His female companion didn't answer, taking the lead into the partially collapsed garage. In truth, she probably didn't know what the hell was going on either. Both she and her younger associate had been apprehended downtown for a number of hours.

Though Ivy's operative hadn't said where. If the street dealers had been pulled off their corners, why had two soldiers been left behind? Carson's curiosity had always gotten the better of him. He'd never been able to look an answer straight in the face without questioning the premise. It was one of the reasons the FBI had brought him on board. Why they'd trusted him to go into this assignment.

He followed in his companion's tracks through debris, pools of water and what looked like pulverized cement toward the entrance into the building. One point of entry. One point of exit. He gauged the chances of being able to turn back now and scanned the property over one shoulder. They weren't looking good. "So how did Socorro get the drop on you two?"

"It was stupid, really." She led him into the building, and a sensation of being crushed took hold, with a healthy hint of resistance. Though his companion kept moving as though they couldn't possibly die within these walls. "We were on a stakeout, and my phone died. We didn't get the word about pulling back until it was too late."

"A stakeout?" Carson hadn't received a single order the past month, but apparently, that wasn't the case for the rest of the soldiers he'd served beside. It didn't make sense. Someone was still operating the cartel despite the limited resources and manpower, and yet they'd managed to pull this many soldiers out of thin air. His gut clenched tighter with each step he took deeper into the belly of the building. He took the time to memorize the route they were taking through the maze of corridors. Or maybe *Sangre por Sangre* wasn't as injured as upper management wanted everyone to believe. "Whereabouts?"

"Across the street from that Socorro bitch's apartment. The one who runs the place." She slowed her pace. Just enough to maneuver behind him in the narrow corridor. "We were told there was a potential rat in our ranks, and that he would be there. Our orders were to drag him back to face his punishment."

Carson scanned the hallway up ahead. They hadn't come in contact with anyone else from the cartel, but his instincts said the moment they did, he was out of options. He slipped his hand into his opposite pocket, out of his companion's sight, and secured Ivy's pocketknife in his palm. He hadn't meant to hold on to it, but the chaos of the two days since the battle in the salvage yard had prioritized more important things. "You got a name of this rat?"

"Funny you should mention it," she said. "Because I was told it was you."

She didn't hesitate to make the first strike. His companion latched on to his shoulder and dug her fingernails into his skin. He arced the pocketknife toward her temple, but there was a reason she'd been recruited into *Sangre por Sangre*. Her background in street fighting had only served her when cornered. She blocked his attack. Carson took the opportunity to go for the other side of her head.

Max's barks filled the hallway and threatened to trigger a ringing in his ears from her proximity. She waited for her turn to attack, but he wouldn't give the order. Not yet.

His fist connected with the soft tissue of his companion's cheekbone. He brought his heel up and kicked straight into her chest.

She fell back into the corridor wall, sliding down until she hit the ground. Out of breath.

"Come on, Max. We gotta get the hell out of here." Carson didn't wait for his companion to get back up. He bolted back the way they'd come, playing through each turn they'd taken in his head. Except there seemed to be no end to this place. He picked up the pace. The cartel's top brass knew he'd handed intel from within the organization to Socorro. They knew about his relationship with Ivy. And if they were waiting for him at her apartment, they'd most likely intended to use her to punish him. "Where the hell is the exit?"

This was the way they'd come. He was sure of it. Only now...

A barrage of flashlights assaulted his vision as he took the next turn.

Carson pulled up short, though every cell in his body screamed for him to turn around. He brought one hand up to block the brightness of the flashlights, but his vision refused to adjust. It was no use. They had him pinned. Going back would only extend the inevitable.

Max made her discontent known almost instantly, her low growl threatening anyone who dared touch her handler.

"Dominic, you made it." An outline shifted forward through the wall of individual lights. And presumably the weapons trained on him. Sebastian had somehow remained in one piece. Considering the beating Carson had given him, his quick recovery only credited the complicated design to the mask the cartel soldier seemed to wear. This was no ordinary recruiter for a drug cartel. Carson didn't know what the hell he was. "We were getting worried."

This was it. The moment he'd dreaded for two years. His cover had been blown, and there was no going back. Not to Socorro. Not to the cartel. Not even to the FBI.

They'd all abandoned him. But, worse, he'd abandoned them. The power of knowing an entire organization—that a partner—had his back in case the cartel had learned of his true identity wasn't there anymore. He was on his own.

"Sorry I'm late." He tried to count the soldiers at Sebastian's back through the shadows. Too many for him to number. Too many for him to fight alone. His blood ran hot at the idea of dying right here in this place. With nothing but his weapon and Ivy's pocketknife on him. And Max. She'd be forced to watch before Sebastian had her put down and buried somewhere nobody would find her remains. Hell, she deserved better than this. "Hell of a party you're throwing."

"All in your honor, my friend. Please." Sebastian angled one side of his body, completely at ease with the potential of an attack. In fact, Carson had the feeling the son of a bitch was betting on it. "Join us, won't you? This moment has been coming for a long time."

Carson didn't have a choice. He scanned the walls, clutching on to Ivy's pocketknife—just to have something to keep him in the moment—and took a single step forward.

Pain splintered across the back of his skull.

He fell forward, losing his grip on the pocketknife, and hit the floor on all fours. Lightning didn't come close to describing the patterns exploding behind his eyes. Max's revolt went into overdrive as she lunged at his attacker. Loud screams pierced through the haze closing in around Carson's mind. He couldn't think, couldn't force his limbs to obey his commands.

"Enough," Sebastian said.

A single shot sucked the life out of Carson.

The K-9's whimper etched into his brain and refused to let up. Then silence. It bounced off the cinder-block walls and dug deeper holes into his heart. His pulse rocketed higher as rage spread hot and thick through his veins. Carson shot to his feet, turning on his heel. His fist connected with the soldier who'd clocked him. The man dropped hard beside Max's still frame. "No!"

His knees couldn't hold his weight anymore as grief overwhelmed any thought of his own survival. Carson pressed his face into Max's, and she licked at the tears. She was alive. For now. He skimmed his hand down the length of her body, coming away with blood. He'd done this to her. He'd trained her to protect him, and now... Now he was going to lose her.

Fingers fisted into his hair and pulled him away from his partner.

"I'm sorry to say dogs are not invited to this fiesta." Sebastian dragged him across the dirt and tossed him back onto the front lines of infantry ready to fire.

Flashlights danced around Carson as he looked up at the man who'd brought him into the cartel. A man whose life he'd saved. "I'm going to kill you for that. Every single one of you."

Sebastian's knees popped as he crouched beside him.

Fisting another handful of hair, the cartel leader forced Carson's head back. The physical damage from their brawl had darkened, sharpening some features and downplaying others on the older man's face. "You asked me to give my bosses a message the last time I saw you. Consider your message delivered, Agent Lang."

Chapter Thirteen

She'd already lost one of her operatives.

She couldn't lose another.

Ivy massaged her uninjured palm into the steering wheel, but no amount of distraction could take away from the desperation clawing through her chest. Carson had made his choice to go back to the cartel in an effort to warn the friends he'd made of the danger headed their way. She should let him deal with the consequences of that choice. But she couldn't. She couldn't leave him to Sebastian's sadism. She couldn't let him suffer as she had in that small room at the salvage yard.

She was angry with him—more than she'd been when he'd taken this assignment—but that didn't mean she'd stopped caring about him. Loving him. Nobody, not even her worst enemy, deserved that kind of pain. She'd watched her mother endure it for years and had finally gotten the strength to put it to a stop. It had taken everything she had, and she wouldn't give anything less now.

Because she loved him.

Because the best thing she could do with this life was to protect someone else. But Carson hadn't seen her devotion to stop the pain of this world from touching those she cared about as selfless. His accusation, that she bulldozed everyone and everything in her path to get what she wanted, had left her feeling carved out and empty. She'd known what her former partners had thought of her. She'd heard their whispers and knew about their transfer requests. With Carson...she'd been different. She'd let him through her guard. She'd smiled more. She'd laughed. Their banter had kept her from spiraling into the nightmares of the past, and his touch had kept her warm.

But old habits died hard.

She could see where she'd messed up, like a long line of dominoes. Tip the first one and the others were bound to feed into the final outcome. The end of their partnership had been coming for a long time. The wrong turns she'd taken were clear as day as she looked back. By not fighting his acceptance of the undercover assignment. By keeping her distance when he'd brought back intel to Socorro. By telling him her safety and health weren't his concern. It was all there, staring back at her in a mirror of failure. She'd just been too late to put a stop to the final domino from falling.

"You're going to tear that steering wheel in half if you keep it up." Granger Morais kept his attention straight forward, his laptop open as he provided the GPS info on their stolen SUV. But she already knew where they were headed. No matter what the tracking said. "We're about a mile out."

"We're not going for the SUV. Send the coordinates for *Sangre por Sangre*'s headquarters to the rest of the team." She targeted each of the SUVs in her rearview mirror. Four vehicles in total with two police cruisers in the rear. She'd tried to convince Chief Halsey to stay with Jocelyn, but there'd been no persuading the man from getting his pound of flesh. Sebastian would regret the day he'd put his hands on one of her operatives.

The cartel would see them coming from a mile away. That was the point. To take a stand. To make a point. That nobody messed with Socorro Security.

"You're sure that's where this ends?" Granger was looking at every angle, every possibility. The idea of them showing up to an empty building was probably the worst that could happen in his eyes.

She directed her attention to the SUV up ahead. Angled off the side of the road. Abandoned. Except somewhere in the back of her mind she realized someone would've had to have driven it out into the middle of the desert. Someone most likely waiting to ambush them. "More sure than I've been about anything else in my life."

Ivy grabbed for the radio velcroed to the dashboard and hit the talk button. She'd had Alpine Valley PD tuned in to their private channel in case they got separated. "We're coming up on our stolen SUV. Be prepared to take on fire."

Granger reached into the back seat and pulled his Kevlar from beside his bull terrier, Zeus. The dog was more fat than muscle, but when it came to protecting his handler, the K-9 never failed. Mostly by sitting on anyone who dared get close enough. The counterterrorism agent threaded himself into his gear. He leaned forward in his seat, studying their SUV through the windshield, then took the radio and opened the line. "Movement. Passenger side, back wheel well. Scarlett, that's all you."

"Understood." The security consultant's voice crackled through the line.

Ivy sped past the sitting SUV, then watched as Scarlett hung back and let Alpine PD, Jones and Cash pass. The SUV at the rear of the pack moved out of line.

Then the shooting started. The cartel soldier presumably responsible for ditching the SUV opened fire on the caravan. Bullets thudded against Ivy's back window but didn't penetrate, thanks to bulletproof glass and armored panels.

Scarlett's vehicle suddenly sped up.

And targeted the back quarter panel of the abandoned SUV. The security consultant rammed her vehicle straight into the other. The cartel soldier was caught by the collision and thrown clear.

"What the hell is she doing? I wanted her to trigger the explosive. Not ram the other vehicle." Slowing, Ivy brought the rest of the vehicles to a halt to assess the situation. She forced her upper body to turn in her seat. Waiting. The driver's-side airbag had deployed in the rear vehicle.

"Guess Scarlett has her own ideas of what qualifies as 'that's all you.'" Granger didn't seem surprised. Or worried. It was his calm nature that would get her through what was to come. "See? She's fine."

Ivy caught sight of her operator punching down the airbag. Scarlett shouldered out of the vehicle, not an inch worse for wear. In fact, a wide smile had taken over the security consultant's expression as she hitched a ride in one of the other vehicles. Ivy turned back to the road. "I need to up her liability insurance."

The radio staticked. "Am I supposed to ignore the fact Scarlett intentionally rammed another vehicle and most likely killed everyone inside?" Chief Halsey asked.

Ivy nodded to the radio. "That's all you, Morais."

Her counterterrorism operative fisted the radio. "Yes." One word. End of conversation.

The hum of tires on dirt worked to settle her nerves as they approached *Sangre por Sangre*'s headquarters, but she couldn't trust that feeling. Not yet. Not until they had a clear read on the situation and Carson's location. "Remember the priority."

"I got it." Granger thumbed bullets into the magazine of his pistol, laptop now angled sideways at his feet. "Get Lang out. Make sure Sebastian doesn't leave. Easy as…Jocelyn's homemade chocolate chip cookies."

"Have you seen the amount of ingredients that goes into those?" she asked. "They are not easy. But, damn, are they worth the wait."

He didn't respond right away, the pressure of his attention boring into her as strong and slow as an oil drill.

"She's going to be okay, Ivy. Jocelyn is strong," he said. "She'll be back in the field in no time."

Ivy's grip tightened all over again. "But will she forgive me for putting her in the crosshairs in the first place?"

Granger didn't seem to have an answer to that.

A chain-link fence materialized as they drew closer to the massive man-made crater protecting the cartel's hideout. It was a forty-five-degree angle down, but Ivy had prepared for this. "Hold on to something."

She pressed the accelerator as Granger grabbed for the dash. They closed the distance between them and the flimsy barrier and blew straight through it. Sparks lit up as metal met metal, but the fence had never stood a chance against her vehicle.

The SUV instantly dipped over the edge and down into the bowl. Gravity lost its hold on Ivy's stomach as they plummeted toward the basin. Four vehicles followed behind, all catching air as they launched over the rim and down. Her team had chosen to follow her into the depths of hell, and she would never forget it.

Ivy twisted the wheel as the SUV hit flat earth and got out of the way of the convoy behind. Within seconds of touchdown, bodies started appearing through the wide field of cars preventing them from driving straight to the front door.

Another round of bullets bounced off the vehicle.

Granger shoved the magazine into his weapon as he fought to stay upright from the wicked turns she was forced to make. "Head for the garage. It's the easiest way in."

She forced the SUV into a skid in order to get as close as possible to the entry point. All four vehicles behind her did the same, setting up a semicircle of protection.

The radio lit up. "Get inside. Alpine Valley PD will cover you. We got this." Chief Halsey's insistence told her he was all too happy to pick off as many cartel soldiers as he could.

Ivy responded. "Copy that. Try not to get shot."

"Can't promise anything, but I'll keep it in mind." Halsey's patrol cruiser lit up, his voice registering over the PA. "This is Alpine Valley police. Put your weapons down and your hands on your heads. No? Okay, then."

Return fire thumped through the windows.

Ivy and Granger took advantage. She unholstered her weapon, using only her free index finger to go for the latch, and kicked the door open. The driver's-side door protected her from the spray of gunfire. She couldn't advance until the bullets stopped. She couldn't get to Carson and Max.

A length of silence punctured through her raised senses. She nodded at Granger over the hood of the SUV. "Go."

Ivy pumped her legs as fast as they would go. The stitches in her side screamed and stretched, threatening to tear from the effort, but she wouldn't stop. Not until she found her partner. They made it to the overhang of the garage and ran straight into shadow. It took a few seconds for her vision to adjust, but she refused to slow down.

"This way." Granger took the lead as Jones, Scarlett and Cash brought up the rear with their K-9s in tow. All free of bullet holes.

"I was really hoping I would never have to come back here," Jones said.

Cash moved to Ivy's left side. As though they'd each taken position as her personal bodyguard. "Imagine how I feel. I blew this place to hell and back with C-4, and it's somehow still standing."

"Did you use the right amount? You've got to get the measurements right or it does no good at all. I've told you that a dozen times." Scarlett was a little too buoyant for someone who'd just sent a cartel soldier flying through the air.

"Quiet." Granger pulled up short at the single entry into the building. He raised a hand, beckoning them forward.

Scarlett's twin Dobermans rushed through the door, and the other K-9s fought to catch up.

The team moved as one into the darkened corridor, and a dampness she didn't want to think about slipped beneath her blazer. "This place is worse than you guys wrote in your reports."

"You have no idea." Jones switched the flashlight mounted to his pistol on. "I got something over here. Oh, hell."

"What is it?" It took Ivy a second to get a visual as all four of her operatives crowded around some kind of mass in the middle of the floor. The K-9s were whining, shifting on their feet and circling. She saw the fur first. Then the watery black eyes staring up at her. Unblinking. Her stomach flipped as she lunged to put pressure on the German shepherd's blood-matted fur. "Get Chief Halsey in here! Now!"

So THIS WAS what dying felt like.

Carson's head skimmed the cement underneath him. Above him? He couldn't think straight. Whatever direction, there was no getting out of the mess he'd put himself in. Strung up by his ankles. Surrounded by armed gunmen willing to pull the trigger with a single word. Nope. He wasn't going anywhere. Not without a miracle, and he didn't see Ivy and her team showing him any kind of grace when they burned this place to the ground.

Blood coated the inside of his mouth. He'd lost one of his back molars during the many fists to his face. Turned out Sebastian had been hiding more than his true identity all this time. An aging old man, he was not. No. There was a contained strength hidden within the cartel recruiter's bones. Something Carson had never imagined.

And, damn it, he hurt. Everywhere. He spit the next rush of blood to clear his mouth. "Bet it feels good to finally be yourself, Sebastian. Hunting and killing those women must've been too easy."

Except the son of a bitch hadn't gone easy on Ivy. He'd done this to her. Tortured her, humiliated her, nearly killed her. Would have if she hadn't bested Sebastian with her training and will to live.

"Easy?" Sebastian wiped his bloodied hands on the shirt of another soldier on the periphery. His voice almost echoed off the open two-story cinder block that had taken too much damage over the years. "No. Those women, they fought. They begged. They made it fun. You? I just want to kill you."

It was the same room the war correspondent had been brought into and tormented for information concerning photos she'd taken over a period of three days—evidence of the cartel working in cahoots with a state senator. Carson had been powerless to stop it, and so he'd volunteered to take the place of her abusers. Holding back his strikes without giving away his intentions. He'd at least given her the chance to regain some of her strength, to escape. Thankfully, one of Socorro's operatives had helped her survive. "Then what's the holdup? You know who I am. You know what I've been doing inside *Sangre por Sangre* all these years. Why wait?"

Blood rushed to his head, darkening his vision. Lack of sleep. Lack of nutrients. Heartbreak. Possibly a concussion. They would all play a vital role in the next hours.

Sebastian finished cleaning his busted knuckles and turned his attention back to Carson with nothing but death in his eyes. "You know, I never married. Never had children. Building this organization took everything I had. The lieutenants I recruited became family. My soldiers, my children. We worked together to bring about change. To finally take what was stolen from us so long ago."

Sangre por Sangre's founder—Carson still couldn't wrap his head around that—withdrew a blade from one of the soldiers looking on. He moved faster than Carson expected. The blade stabbed through Carson's upper arm. His scream failed to drown out Sebastian's words. "Every single soldier I've lost in the past two years was because of you. Men and women who devoted their lives to my cause, who fought for me, bled for me and died for me. You're going to pay for their lives. Slowly. Painfully. Then I'm going to leave your body in the desert for Agent Bardot to find. Then I'm going to kill another of her operatives. Then another.

Until she has nobody left, and she'll know the pain that you two have caused me."

Excruciating pain burned until it overrode every sense Carson owned. He lost his control to the point a laugh escaped his chest. It rolled through him, gaining strength, blocking out the pain. Blood dripped beneath his shirtsleeve and tendriled over his collarbone.

"This is funny to you?" Sebastian asked.

"This? No." Carson tried to shake his head. "I'm just imagining what Ivy's going to do to you. Especially if she finds out you shot her dog. You have no idea the kind of hell you've brought down on yourself. On the soldiers you claim to care about. You think you're some kind of protector. You have no idea what that word means compared to her. And I can't wait to see you fall."

A fist rocketed into his face. Carson's body swung away from his attacker, then back for another strike. His head snapped back. Pain unlike anything he'd experienced before kept him conscious and urged his body to shut down at the same time.

He wouldn't be able to take much more.

But of all the ways to go, he'd choose this a thousand times more. Because he knew the end result in his bones. He knew that Ivy would finish the assignment they'd started while they'd still been partners in the FBI. Despite his betrayal, she would remain the same woman she'd always been.

Valiant. Committed. Courageous.

He'd never been any of those things. Not like her. Carson had taken the easy way out. He saw that now.

How going undercover within the cartel gave him the mask of hero, but Ivy had been on the outside. Fighting. Risking her team and her reputation and her own life. She'd earned a target on her back to protect him. How hadn't he seen it before?

Their last conversation played on repeat at the back of his mind. He'd accused her of doing it all for herself. For the glory, to keep building a wall between her and the rest of the world, but that couldn't have been farther from the truth. She was brave. Braver than Carson. He'd believed her inability to separate herself from their investigations over the years had built her into an unyielding, closed-off partner, but that wasn't the case at all. The hell she'd suffered as a kid had led her to use her work to distract herself from dealing with the trauma. The grief. At ten years old, she'd had to shoot a man who beat her and her mother. How could he have seen her intensity as anything more than a way to ensure she never had to suffer like that again? That all she needed was for someone to choose her? Ivy Bardot loved fiercely. The proof was right there in the two bullets still cataloged in evidence in her stepfather's investigation box. She risked everything in pursuit of holding on to the people who meant the most to her.

And he'd done the stupid thing and turned his back on her. He'd become a coward, so different from the times he'd come home with a black eye or a bloody lip because he'd refused to back down from the bullies who made fun of his mixed race.

Because he'd just wanted Ivy to choose him, too. To love him as much as he loved her. Losing his mother had taken everything from him, but Ivy had been there to step into that role of companion. And when he'd gone undercover and lost his constant connection to her, he'd tried to replace it with the very men and women who would kill him with a single order now. To live up to her expectations.

He'd relied on other people to love and support him without ever considering he could do it himself. That he was the one responsible for his own happiness. Not his mother. Not Ivy. Not the people he'd convinced himself could give him what he needed from within the cartel. Him. The realization hit him harder than Sebastian's next fist. And he wanted to figure out how to fix it. To move forward without that external validation. For once, he wanted to find out what made him happy. Other people's interests be damned.

Only that seemed impossible now. Hanging upside down in the middle of a drug cartel headquarters surrounded by soldiers ready to kill him.

"Unfortunately, I'm not the one who will be falling today, Agent Lang." Sebastian nodded to one of the soldiers off to one side. His female companion stepped forward. "Get him ready. I expect Socorro is already on its way, and we don't want to keep them waiting."

Socorro. Ivy. Carson pulled at the rope binding his hands behind his back with everything he had left. Which wasn't much. The threads didn't even stretch as the cartel soldier waved two more companions closer to assist. "You knew who I was. All this time. You knew what I was doing."

"Of course I knew," Sebastian said. "How else was

I supposed to keep an eye on my old friend Agent Bardot?"

Son of a bitch. Carson had served within the cartel to provide Ivy and her team a leg up in this war, but he'd only been Sebastian's puppet. Putting Ivy and Socorro in danger. Drawing them into a trap. "You can't win this, Sebastian. It doesn't matter how many soldiers you throw at them or how many guns you buy. She won't stop until you're behind bars or six feet under."

Sebastian wiped blood from the blade used to stab Carson's arm on the same rag he'd used to clean his hands. "Don't worry about me, my friend. There's a reason I lured those Socorro dogs here."

"What are you talking about?" Carson struggled as three soldiers braced his shoulders and started hauling him down. The world righted itself as they held him upright. They maneuvered him toward the corridor. Three to one wasn't good odds.

"Let's just say my focus is no longer on keeping operations moving or making more money. I've moved beyond mere survival." The cartel founder smiled, easy and relaxed, despite the monster hidden within. "It's all about the future now. I must thank you, Agent Lang. Without you, I never would've learned the identities of Socorro's operatives, their protocols, their weapons preferences. You will be the reason *Sangre por Sangre* lives on to fight another day. Thank you."

Carson hadn't provided any of that.

"You son of a bitch." He fought the strength of three soldiers as they dragged him toward the door. He didn't know where they were taking him. It didn't matter. What mattered was warning Ivy.

"Get him out of here, please." Sebastian rounded a table Carson hadn't noticed until then, turning a laptop toward him. Surveillance footage. Of the complex. And there, on the screen, a line of operatives making their way through the building. Ivy in the lead. "It seems our guests have arrived early. Let's give them a proper greeting, shall we?"

Gunfire punctured through Carson's shallow breathing a split second before Socorro's private military contractors breached the room.

Ivy took aim at the man of the hour as her team and their K-9s filed in behind her. "Who shot my dog!"

Chapter Fourteen

No one raised their hand.

That was okay. She would find the person who shot Max. She would tear this whole building down to do it, too. Until then, Chief Halsey was taking care of the German shepherd the best way he could. She lost count of the number of soldiers taking aim at her and her team. One wrong move. That was all it would take to tear apart both of their organizations. Ivy raised her weapon, at Sebastian. "I'm going to give you one chance to put your weapons down and surrender."

"You must be confused, Agent Bardot." Sebastian's laugh inspired the rest of his soldiers to participate. He spread his arms wide, motioning to the men and women prepared to shoot on his order. "You see, I have far more manpower. You, you have four operatives and some dogs."

"You're right. Doesn't feel like a fair fight, does it?" Ivy scanned the room. Instantly landing on Carson. He'd been bound, beaten. Blood dripped down his arm and slid between his fingers. "Would you like to invite more soldiers to come help you? We'll wait."

Sebastian's smile slipped off his face. He stepped

away from the desk he'd put between him and her team. "You've been hunting me for two years. Sent your lapdog to identify me, to undermine my operation. You send your operatives to take out my lieutenants. All while you hide in your black tower. You are not ready for what's coming, little girl. You are not strong enough to fight me."

Strong enough. When the hell had she let other people determine what she was capable of? When had she let it haunt her to the point of paralysis? Ivy lowered her weapon. "Shall we finish what we started in that basement, Sebastian? You, me. No federal agents. No cartel soldiers to interfere. That's what you want, right? To prove *Sangre por Sangre* deserves to sit on the throne. That all of this leads to one outcome—you standing over the bodies of your enemies. I'll give you that chance."

"Ivy, what the hell are you doing?" Carson struggled to be free of his captives. In vain.

"I would love nothing more." A wide smile transformed the cartel founder's expression. "One weapon. No guns. To the death. I win, I will kill your entire team and your undercover operative. Socorro will be no more."

"And if I win, *Sangre por Sangre* surrenders to the Alpine Valley Police Department and Socorro. Never to operate again." Ivy passed her weapon to Granger, positioned behind her.

"Boss, you sure about this?" Scarlett kept her voice low, but the concern was louder than anything else in the room. "You're still injured from the last time you two were in a room together."

"I'll be fine. I have something he doesn't." Her gaze cut to Carson as she stripped out of the sling meant to help her dislocated shoulder heal.

"What's that?" Jones seemed to take inventory of the soldiers he would like to take out, that battle-ready energy coming off him in waves.

She handed off the sling to Granger and rolled her shoulder out. "A team who has my back, no matter what. As long as I have you guys, I can never lose. But for him? Every single one of these soldiers will put their own survival first if pushed." Ivy turned to face Sebastian as his soldiers cleared away the desks and debris from the middle of the room. "See the C-4 strapped to the major structural beams overhead? He's not confident in his plan to get to the rest of you. He plans on bringing down the building on top of us if this doesn't go his way. Make sure he fails. Understand?"

"I have some experience with that," Scarlett said. "I'll take care of it."

"Granger, Jones, Cash." She didn't want to say goodbye. She didn't want to admit that this was a bad idea and that she had no way of knowing if her reason would hold up against a man who'd already killed four women and put another in the hospital. Not to mention the thousands of lives his organization had taken over the years when Socorro had failed to protect the people they swore to protect. "The moment he attacks, he's going to let his soldiers have a field day. Don't let your guards down. And feel free to take as many of them out as you can. Just make sure Carson isn't one of them."

"Wait. Are we friends with this guy again?" Cash said.

"Enough waiting." Sebastian kicked a rock from in front of his foot. She'd misjudged him in the dark of a salvage yard before, then again when her eye had swollen to the point she hadn't been able to see. The man had claimed to spend twenty years building his empire, but there was still a youthfulness to him. A strength she hadn't considered before.

This was going to hurt. But the past no longer had a hold on her. All that mattered was the future. Hers. Her team's. And Carson's. Ivy shrugged out of her blazer and handed it off to Granger. The muscles in her shoulder still ached. The stitches in her side warned her not to take another step, but she wasn't doing this to feed some ego-driven show of dominance. This was how she protected her family. Just as she'd done all those years ago.

Ivy took a literal and metaphorical step into the ring. "Sure you want to go through with this, Sebastian? That shoulder of yours isn't looking too good."

His laugh slid beneath her confidence and started to break it up into pieces. "How's the side, Agent Bardot?"

She didn't want to give away the pain she was already in. Not to him. Filling her lungs with as much oxygen as they could hold, she steadied her pulse with Carson in her peripheral vision.

"Ivy, you don't have to do this. You don't have to—" Her partner's words were cut short from the sucker punch to his gut. He doubled over within his captor's grasp.

Sebastian was the first to strike. He took advantage of her distraction and launched at her. She saw him coming.

Ivy fisted his collar and rammed her forehead straight into his nose. The son of a bitch fell backward and hit the floor.

All hell broke loose.

Bullets sprayed across the room. Her team broke apart, each operative hunting for cover. Cash returned fire as his rottweiler, Bear, ran straight for the nearest soldier.

Ivy threw herself behind Sebastian's desk. A soldier reached over the edge. He grabbed on to her tank top and pulled her across the surface. A knife arced down toward her face. She managed to lean out of the way, letting it embed in the wood. Gripping the handle, she pulled it free and returned it to its owner. Straight into his chest. The soldier fell back, and she got to her feet.

Two more came for her. Both tried to cage her between them, but she was faster. Ivy ducked out from the reach of one and kicked his knee out from under him. The soldier slammed into the floor face-first. The other got a good hold on her from behind. Locking her arms behind her. Her shoulder threatened to dislocate all over again.

"None of you are getting out of here alive." Sebastian stumbled to his feet. Blood coursed from his nose and framed his mouth. Stained his graying beard. He withdrew a blade from a sheath on his belt.

"And here I thought we were going to play by the rules." Ivy rammed her heel into the soldier's foot at her back. He released his hold and tipped off-balance. He fell at her feet, and she made sure he would never get up again. Kicking her toes into his groin as hard as she could.

Just as Sebastian closed the distance between them.

He slammed into her. The knife grazed the outside of her arm as the cartel founder pinned her against the desk. She latched on to his wrist to gain control, but he was a hell of a lot stronger than he let on. Her shoulder screamed for her to let go. But she couldn't. Not yet.

Time seemed to slow.

Seconds distorted and stretched into minutes. Scarlett took a fist to the face as she tried to reach the laptop dislodged in the chaos. Cash blocked one attack while attempting to dodge a blade to the gut from the opposite direction. Granger had been pinned against the wall by no less than three soldiers. Granger's bellow filled the entire room as Jones used one of the cartel soldiers as a shield to avoid getting shot.

And Carson. He'd shoved one of his captors off but failed to account for the soldier at his back. The butt of a weapon slammed down onto his skull. His legs collapsed out from underneath him.

They were losing. They were going to fail. Because of her. Because maybe her stepfather—maybe Sebastian— had been right. Maybe she wasn't strong enough to win this war. But she wouldn't stop trying.

"Look at them, Agent Bardot. See them suffer." Sebastian struggled to bring the knife down into her heart. Sweat dripped from his forehead and splashed onto her face. "I can make it all go away. All you have to do is give in."

The tip of the blade penetrated through her tank top. She couldn't hold him off much longer. A pinprick of pain registered just below her collarbone. "I gave my word to those women."

Ivy arched her hips off the desk and threw his weight to one side. Sebastian had no choice but to follow. She hiked his wrist upward, then straight down onto the edge of the desk. The crunch of bone pierced through the sound of gunfire and screams. Along with his scream. He stared up at her with nothing but violence and death.

"I was going to make you pay for what you did to them." Ivy kicked Sebastian's legs out from under him. Fisting his collar while he was down, she ignored the pain in her shoulder. And launched her fist into his face. Once. Twice. His head snapped back. Years of being told she wasn't strong enough to fight created a new energy that sizzled through her. "I keep my promises."

Sebastian's body went limp in her grasp. His eyes rolled back in his head. Unconscious. Ivy let him sink to the floor. It was over. The loss. The pain. The fear. Straightening, she left the cartel's founder there to suffer the consequences that had led them to this room.

The gunfire seemed to cease all at once as *Sangre por Sangre* came to terms with the end result. Jones ripped out of a soldier's hold, then pinned his attacker against the wall. Granger shirked off the three men trying to bring him down. Scarlett didn't seem to notice any change in her surroundings, her focus on the C-4 ready to explode at the touch of a button. Cash shoved one of the soldiers forward.

And Carson raised his gaze to hers through the blood seeping into his eyes. They'd done it. Together. As a team. It had taken so much longer than she'd planned, but they'd—

A gunshot exploded from behind.

Then came the pain. Ivy lowered her attention to the stain spreading across her tank top, then back to her team.

Right before the world went dark.

SOCORRO'S OPERATIVES FELL into action.

Each running to catch their boss before she met the ground.

Carson could only watch Ivy as she fell. The past superimposed the present as he simultaneously saw her collapse in the salvage yard warehouse and hit the floor now. Sebastian lowered his gun hand. A smile creased the outer edges of his face.

Carson's head pounded in rhythm with his increasing heart rate. He could barely see through the blood dripping into his eyes, but struggled to his feet. The soldiers on either side of him fought to keep him down. Under control. It wouldn't work. A fire had started burning in him, and there was nothing anybody could do to put it out. No one but Ivy.

Carson rammed his shoulder into the nearest captor, throwing the son of a bitch off-balance. His female companion he'd gotten out of Socorro holding rushed at him. She didn't make it. He buried his heel in her stomach and took the air right out of her. Her knees dropped as she gasped for breath. Movement registered in his peripheral vision. Carson ducked to avoid the butt of the weapon coming at his face and swung around in time to let the soldier's momentum carry him into another moving in to subdue him.

A third attacker came straight at him. The bastard hiked his foot up as though to land a solid kick. Only Carson managed to capture the soldier's boot between his bound arm and rib cage. One tight jerk and the soldier's ankle practically broke off in Carson's grip. He forced the attacker to hop on one foot, angling the gunman right into another threat.

Pain spidered down Carson's back as a fourth soldier swung his weapon down. It gave *Sangre por Sangre* a chance to gang up on him. Two more attackers grabbed for his shoulders and arms. He took down another coming from the front and took out the soldier's knee. Carson ducked out from the son of a bitch on the left and crushed his head into the soldier's temple. Then had to quickly dodge a knife aimed straight for his spine. The bladesman overcorrected his momentum. But not in time to avoid Carson's knee to his face.

Men and women groaned at his feet. But the fight wasn't over.

Ivy's operatives were dragging her off the battlefield, toward the exit. She hadn't moved, hadn't opened her eyes. Even if she managed to survive, there was no telling when Sebastian would come for her again. Come for her team.

Carson had to end this now.

He caught sight of the cartel's fearless leader making a break for a door he'd once mapped as a secret escape from the building. Low-level soldiers had been kept in the dark. It was just like upper management to sacrifice the men and women they'd used to do their dirty work while keeping their own hands clean. "Sebastian!"

Carson crouched to pick up a fallen knife and sliced through the rope at his wrists. Blood rushed back into his fingertips as he followed after the man responsible for so much death. He'd been an idiot to believe there was an ounce of good within the cartel, that the people at the bottom were simply following orders. He'd been manipulated, used.

And now he was going to make sure it never happened to anyone else.

He dodged another attempt to slow him down. A second soldier pointed a gun at him, but one of Socorro's K-9s—a husky—intercepted and took the gunman down. Fierce growls let him know these dogs weren't in the mood for playing. They were here to protect their handlers. Well, except maybe for the one sitting on top of a cartel soldier off to his right. The bull terrier simply grinned at him as Carson cut across the body-strewn space. And, hell, he couldn't blame the K-9 for adding a bit of fun to this mess. Sometimes that was the only way to make it through the hard stuff.

Ten feet. Five.

Sebastian ducked through the door and secured it behind him.

Just as Carson lunged. His shoulder made contact, but the door had locked from the inside. He slammed both palms against what was meant to look like cinder block, but the exit wouldn't budge. "Sebastian! You coward! You can't run forever! I will find you!"

This was no time for caution. He had to get in there.

"We can help you with that, Lang," a voice said from behind.

Carson turned to find two Socorro operatives, armed to the teeth and not an ounce of exhaustion etched into their faces. To be fair, they hadn't been tortured for a couple of hours. He motioned them forward. Though he wasn't sure of their names, they each had the look of determination of seeing this through to the end. The same determination that had possessed him since coming back to the cartel. "By all means, be my guests."

The one he was fairly certain was called Cash— Socorro's forward scout—raised his weapon and took aim. Then fired. Once. Twice. The second operative— Jones, maybe—rammed the heel of his boot and forced the exit open. "You come for one of us, you come for all of us. Ivy says you're one of us. So go get that son of a bitch. We've got everything covered here."

One of them. Three words shouldn't have held so much weight, but Carson felt the beginnings of the support he'd been searching for all this time. First, with his mother, then through Ivy, and when he'd been required to distance himself from her, from the cartel. Only the people he'd fought beside in the field hadn't ever really felt the same for him as he had for them. It had all been a manipulation. An order. He saw the truth now. He knew what the future held and whom he wanted in his life, and it sure as hell wasn't *Sangre por Sangre*. The haze of revenge and rage lowered to a simmer as he processed the body count. Every Socorro operative was still standing. Apart from Ivy. "Thank you."

"Hey, Lang, hold up," Jones said. "There's something you should know about Socorro. We never go anywhere without our partners."

Both men parted, letting a stubborn, bleeding, protective Ivy through. She held on to her side. Blood seeped between her fingers.

"What the hell are you doing? You were shot." He reached for her, unsure if she would appreciate the contact. "You need medical attention."

Somehow she'd lost even more color since she'd confronted him in Socorro's headquarters. "When have I ever let a wound slow me down? Besides, I may have played up the seriousness of the shot." She pulled her hand away, revealing a stained tank top. "There was no way I was going to be able to fight Sebastian on my own with a dislocated shoulder and a stab wound. So I let him take me out of the equation."

Disbelief stole the air from his lungs. "But the bullet—"

"Was very real." Her laugh took the tension out of his shoulders. She was alive. She was okay. Ivy lifted the edge of her shirt, showing off a line of blood and burned skin. "But it was just a graze."

"You guys know the longer you stand here, the farther our suspect gets, right?" Cash pointed toward the door.

Ivy set clear green eyes on Carson, and the entire world seemed to make sense again. As though for the first time in two years, he'd given himself permission to make his desires known instead of bowing out to everyone else's. "Are you ready to end this?"

"Let's do this." Carson shoved through the door. His

heart rocketed into his throat every step he stumbled in the darkness. Grief charged through him at the realization he didn't have Max to help guide him with her higher senses. Except he wasn't entirely on his own.

He had his partner.

"I've never been through this corridor before." Carson felt his way along the wall, following the sharp turns that seemed to never end. "This must've been how the cartel was still able to operate over the past few months."

"Where does it go?" she asked.

He didn't have a chance to answer as sunlight pierced into the darkened space up ahead. "I'm guessing outside." Carson offered her his hand. Which she took. "Come on."

Ivy unholstered her weapon—the same one she'd handed off to one of her operatives earlier—as they ran. They left the protection of the building and scanned the open desert. "Where did he—"

An engine revved from their left.

And shot directly at them.

Carson pulled Ivy with him, just as she'd done that night in her apartment when they'd been under attack. Saving his life. They hit the ground as one, and he tucked her into his body. Dirt worked into his mouth and nose with each roll, but they'd avoided dying. For now.

The vehicle crashed into the exit, sealing it off. Sebastian shoved free of the driver's seat, armed with what looked like a long piece of rebar.

Ivy was the first to get to her feet. And took aim. "Drop it, Sebastian. Or I will shoot."

"You took everything from me!" The cartel founder

brought the metal weapon down on her forearm. The gun went off. A bullet shot into the wall of the building and spit dirt.

Ivy fell forward. The gun fell from her hand, out of reach, as she cradled her arm against her chest. Sebastian raised the elongated metal for another strike, and Ivy rolled. The rebar thudded into the cracked earth. "Now I'm going to take everything you love from you."

Carson dragged Ivy to stand, maneuvering her behind him. "It's over, Sebastian. There's nothing left of your cartel. Give yourself up, and you might live another twenty years."

Sebastian unpocketed some kind of device. A small black box with an antenna. A detonator? "Say goodbye to your team, Agent Bardot."

He hit the button.

Except nothing happened.

Carson waited. One second. Two. Sebastian pressed the button again, then once more. And the tension eased out of Carson's shoulders.

"Looking for this?" Scarlett Beam rounded the corner and into view. Tossing a brick of white…C-4? Jones, Cash, Granger and their K-9s followed. Each taking aim with guns in hand. "You can thank Ivy for that. She noted the C-4 wired into the structural beams of the building. I took the opportunity to reprogram your detonator. To mine."

The security consultant showed off her phone. Then tapped the screen with a smile not meant for life-and-death situations.

The explosion started within, bringing the building

in on itself in a series of blasts but containing it at the same time. It was the perfect system.

"You're finished, *el jefe*." Ivy rounded into Sebastian's vision, seemingly memorizing his realization that he'd lost. He'd outmanned and outgunned Socorro, but he couldn't beat them. Because they were a team. "*Sangre por Sangre* is dead."

Sebastian sank to his knees as he watched his headquarters collapse in on itself.

Sirens echoed off the sides of the man-made bowl. A patrol cruiser skidded to a stop behind Carson, and Chief Halsey pulled a set of handcuffs from his pocket.

"Sebastian Aguado, you are under arrest for a whole lot of shit." Halsey pinned Sebastian's arms behind his back and hauled the cartel founder to his feet to install the cuffs. "Namely, coming after my partner, but that one will be the least of your worries. Because you get to ride in the back seat with her German shepherd. We've got two years of charges you've earned. And I'm going to make sure every single one of them sticks."

Carson couldn't help but etch this scene into his brain. To convince him it was real.

Alpine Valley PD shoved Sebastian headfirst into the back seat of the patrol car. Chief Halsey secured the cartel founder inside with a nod in Ivy's direction.

"It's finished." Ivy stared after the cruiser, the sun highlighting the bruises and scrapes along one side of her face. "After two years, we finally took down *Sangre por Sangre*."

Chapter Fifteen

Three days later

She was supposed to feel some kind of relief, wasn't she?

Ivy moved the paperwork that had stacked up over the past week to the other side of her desk. This office had been her command center. She'd stood at this company's helm, given orders and developed strategy to keep her operatives safe and a drug cartel from spreading across the state.

And now? Now she didn't really know what she was supposed to do. A nervous energy urged her to review the dozens of threats that had crossed her desk and pick one to focus on. The Pentagon, of course, was appreciative of her and her team's effort in neutralizing *Sangre por Sangre*, but the cartel had merely been a drop in the bucket. There were a handful of other cartels the DEA, the FBI and the ATF were trying to get a handle on, and not just in the drug arena.

At the same time, the muscles in her shoulder were protesting, and the stitches in her side had torn during the fight three days ago. She hadn't been sleeping since walking away from the cartel's headquarters after Scarlett had finally brought the whole structure down on itself, and her team... Well, they all had families to go home to. Lives to maintain.

She had a bullet-ridden safe house or the couch in her office. She'd gone for the couch the past few nights. The regret had started instantly. Ivy stretched the muscles in her neck on either side. She should replace it with a pullout until the building owner could patch up the holes in her walls. Which, according to him, wouldn't be for another two weeks.

The state prosecutor had made the argument to try Sebastian—actually identified as Silvio Juarez, according to his fingerprints taken in early arrest reports from two decades ago—on a federal level. The US Attorney General was inclined to cut out as many obstacles in the case as possible. Though Ivy was sure Sebastian's lawyers would do their best to slow everything down.

The low-level cartel soldiers who'd managed to survive the final minutes of *Sangre por Sangre*'s demise had been offered deals. Testify against Silvio Juarez or face a life in prison. Most of them had taken the deal. They'd given their statements and signed affidavits negotiating their sentences down to two to three years. It was the best they were going to get. The shooter who'd ambushed her and Carson that first night had admitted to being ordered to shoot Carson if he came into contact with any operatives from Socorro. And considering her partner had waited inside her apartment, the shooter had taken it upon himself to follow through.

Two *Sangre por Sangre* soldiers had admitted to

replacing the couch in Dr. Piel's home after Sebastian had killed her. A deep dive into the physician's background, another pass at her references and interviews with others within Socorro had convinced Ivy of what she'd known from the beginning: Nafessa Piel had not been involved with the cartel. She'd just been the target of a man devoted to making his enemies suffer.

As for the gunman who'd shot Max, his or her identity had yet to come up in Alpine Valley PD's interviews. Whether out of fear or because the cartel soldier hadn't survived, she didn't know. Either way, they would get what they deserved. Max herself was recovering nicely in Socorro's vet clinic. She'd been pampered with top-of-the-line meals, round-the-clock care and all the attention she could possibly want or need.

And Jocelyn was recovering just as well. Though slower than Max. Chief Baker had sent regular updates, but if Ivy knew her logistics coordinator at all, Jocelyn was most assuredly enjoying the time off.

Three knocks pulled her out of convincing herself she should take a look at the case files the Pentagon had sent her way. They wanted her and her team on the next assignment. But something inside of her needed the breather. Two years without a vacation or so much as a night off of being on call had compounded into this...exhaustion. It was something she'd never allowed herself to feel before. But her body wouldn't heal unless she gave it the chance.

Ivy brushed the imaginary wrinkles off her blouse and raised her gaze. And locked on Carson. "Oh. Hi.

I wasn't…" A rush of heat stole her train of thought. "I didn't know you'd been released from the hospital."

The bruises he'd sustained from Sebastian's assault had gone from swollen and dark to a little lighter. The shape of his face had changed slightly, mostly in his nose. Possibly broken. Though she hadn't followed up with him since he'd been taken in one ambulance at the site and she in another. With his wounds fresh, the EMTs had determined the clinic wouldn't be enough. He'd been brought to one of the hospitals in Albuquerque to recover. Fortunately, no one else on the team had been injured. They'd somehow gone up against an entire army and come out the other side unscathed. Apart from the bullet graze along her ribs.

"I checked myself out." Carson stopped at the door. As though he was on his way out. "I couldn't sit there anymore."

"I know how that feels." She traced her fingers over the stack of proposals. Stories of *Sangre por Sangre*'s defeat had hit the media within hours. Mostly thanks to Maggie Caldwell, Jones's partner. Per Ivy's past agreement on all things cartel, the war correspondent had written an exclusive and sold it off to the highest bidder. From there it was just a matter of time. Companies from all over the country, some international, wanted Socorro's expertise in their security needs. "I was going to come visit once I got through these proposals. Not sure if you've heard, but things have been a bit crazy around here."

"I've been watching the news." He took a couple of steps into the office. Studying it while trying not to look at her in the same way he did when faced with a stranger. Was that what they were now? Strangers? A lot had changed in the hours he'd chosen the cartel over siding with her and Socorro. But there had to still be some kind of feeling for her in there, something worth keeping. "Though I was surprised you weren't the one running the press conference."

"I would have been, but I'm still recovering from Sebastian's work. There isn't enough makeup in the world to cover this up." She was trying to make light of the events they'd suffered over the past week, but the humor failed to make her feel any better. Ivy tried to distract this…incompleteness from taking over by moving the files back to the center of her desk. "Granger did well. He's a natural. We've got more contract proposals than we know what to do with. Seems Socorro Security has made a name for itself this week."

Carson seemed to lose his will to keep his distance. In a matter of three steps, he'd rounded her desk. "I didn't come here to talk about Socorro, Ivy. I came here to talk about us."

"Us." The word thrilled her and yet felt so foreign at the same time. There had been a gaping hole in her heart since their conversation in the elevator. The edges were still raw and pulsing, preparing for the next injury. "I contacted the special agent in charge of your undercover assignment. The FBI has closed the investigation into the deaths of the three women we were looking into two years ago. Now that we know Sebastian—Silvio Juarez—killed them and Dr. Piel, your assignment is complete. You are officially released from federal duty, if that's what you want. You're free to go."

"Where am I supposed to go, Ivy?" The regret and heavy dose of sadness deepening his expression pulled at her insides. But this wasn't a decision she could make for him.

She tried to keep her voice light. Tougher than it should've been. Ivy sucked in a deep breath to steady herself and turned back to the files she didn't actually want to go through. To detach herself from the emotion working through her. To give herself a chance to keep the upper hand. "Anywhere you want."

"And what if the place I want to go is home with you?" he asked.

She jerked at the possibility, catching her knuckle on the edge of a piece of paper. The paper cut stung more than the freaking stab wound she'd sustained in the salvage yard. Not really. But close. "Damn it."

Carson was there. Folding her hand between both of his. He swiped the blood rushing to the surface with the pad of his thumb. "I was wrong to believe I could save anyone from the cartel alone, Ivy. I...I thought I'd had something with them that I'd lost with you, and before that with my mother, but it turns out I was being lied to the entire time. I've been seeking this sense of family since my father walked out on us when I was a kid. I wanted that connection with my Hispanic heritage, and I thought I found it with the people I was in the field with. I convinced myself they were just following or-ders like I was, that they didn't have a choice. I was trying to re-create that feeling of having a support system that I missed since going undercover, and I'm sorry."

Her heart sank at the thought of how lonely and isolated he must've felt during his time with the cartel. Just as she had been on the outside. "I'm sorry, too."

Confusion etched three distinct lines between his eyebrows. "You don't have anything to be sorry for."

"Yes, I do." The paper cut didn't hurt so much in his hands. "I chose to delegate intel exchanges between you and Socorro over the past two years. I was afraid if I saw you, I would ask you to give up your assignment and come home. And I knew you would do it because you were my partner, and then all of this would be for nothing, and people would keep dying. So I distanced myself from you. I fed into my isolation to complete this mission, putting everything I had into this company and my team, but all I ended up doing was hurting you. I kept you on the outside the same way I keep other people out, because that's what was easiest. But you deserved so much better. Because I love you."

"I love you, too." His smile broke through the hurt and started to piece her back together, one step at a time. "We're messed up, aren't we?"

"A little bit," she said. "But if I've learned anything over the past week it's been that I need a partner. I need a team. I can't do all of this on my own. I need you. Here, with me, and at home. Where you belong."

"Is that a job offer?" he asked. "Because, to be honest, I think I'm unemployed—"

She kissed him. Totally and deeply. With everything she had. A fury of relief coursed through her veins as

Carson secured her in his arms. The graze on her side put up a little bit of a fight, but she didn't care. He couldn't hurt her. Not as long as they were on the same team. "Welcome back to the land of the living, Agent Lang. From here on out, Dominic Rojas is dead. Think you can handle that?"

"With you at my side, Agent Bardot?" He kissed her again. "I can handle anything."

* * * * *